The Book of Adages, Aphorisms, Idioms, and Colorful Expressions

by James R. Coffey

Illustrations by Amara Kopakova

PublishAmerica
Baltimore

© 2011 by James R. Coffey
All rights reserved. No part of this book may be reproduced, stored in a retrieval system or transmitted in any form or by any means without the prior written permission of the publishers, except by a reviewer who may quote brief passages in a review to be printed in a newspaper, magazine or journal.

First printing

All characters in this book are fictitious, and any resemblance to real persons, living or dead, is coincidental.

PublishAmerica has allowed this work to remain exactly as the author intended, verbatim, without editorial input.

Hardcover 978-1-4626-0091-5
Softcover 978-1-4626-0090-8
PUBLISHED BY PUBLISHAMERICA, LLLP
www.publishamerica.com
Baltimore

Printed in the United States of America

This book is dedicated to my best friend Gary who recognized the need for such a book and that I should be the one to write it, and to my daughter Summer Jessica-Briann, my eternal inspiration.

Table of Contents

CHAPTER ONE 9
(For) all the tea in China 10
(I have) an axe to grind 11
Call a spade a spade 12
Couch potato 13
Dig your own grave 14
(A) dollar to a donut 15
Don't look a gift horse in the mouth........................16
(An) eye for an eye 17
Park your carcass...18
Pitching woo 19
Pull out all the stops......................................20
Royal pain in the ass 21
(Don't go) shootin' your mouth off..........................21
Splitting hairs...22
That hit the spot 24
Turn coat...25
Whole nine yards 26
(A) wink is as good as a nod to a blind horse 28
You're just talkin' outta your ass..........................29

CHAPTER TWO 30
Animal magnetism..31
Born with a silver spoon in their mouth 32
Busy as a one-legged man at an ass-kicking contest..........33
Don't air your dirty laundry 34
Don't be such a nit-picker..................................34
Drunk as a skunk 35
Hair of the dog 36

Hind sight..36
(You couldn't) hit a bear in the ass with a bass fiddle..........37
Keep an eye out..38
(Take a) long walk off a short pier 39
Low man on the totem pole..40
Nose to the grindstone...41
Pay through the nose 41
(It's) raining cats and dogs...42
Shit a brick..42
Take it with a grain of salt...43
Talking Gibberish...44
Two left feet..45

CHAPTER THREE **47**
All haired-over...48
An arm and a leg..48
Apple of my eye...49
Artsy-fartsy..50
Catch a buzz...51
Chew the fat...51
Don't give me no lip..52
Guess what, chicken butt..53
(My) hat's off to you...53
I don't want to hear a peep out of you 54
I'll be dipped in frog shit 55
Nit wit 56
On the cuff..56
Pretty as a picture 58
Put a lid on it..59
Slippery as shit 60
(Give me the) straight poop..61
Sweep it under the rug..61

Wise ass 62
You don't know shit from Shinola 63

CHAPTER FOUR 75
Between you and me and the fence post 76
(You) bet your ass..77
(Wearing your) birthday suit.....................................80
Bosoms 'til Tuesday 81
Bull feathers/horse feathers.......................................81
Caught red handed 82
Chip off the old block 83
Even steven...84
Go suck a toad 85
Hog Heaven..86
Just because there's snow on the roof, doesn't mean there's
   no fire in the furnace..87
Knee-high to a grasshopper 87
No shit, Sherlock 88
Only a paper moon 89
(The) proof is in the pudding 90
Rip, roaring drunk..91
Shoot the moon 92
Stink up a storm...94
Talk is cheap...95
Who let the cat out of the bag..................................95

CHAPTER FIVE 98
Bend over backwards 99
Black balled...99
Bone up 100
Cold as a witch's tit...101
Cut to the chase 102

Dick head 103
Don't get you tits tangles 103
Half past a monkey's ass and a quarter to his balls..............104
Horny as hell..104
Just keep your pants on (You won't be here that long)........105
(A) lick and a promise 105
Lip lock 106
Pussy whipped 107
(A) shit and 2 is 8 and a fart is a fraction..............107
Shoot a beaver 107
Son of a bitch..109
Stroke the mule...109
Sympathy sex...110
Tube steak 111
Wild hair up your ass...112

CHAPTER ONE:

"Moments in History"

Some of the more interesting, insightful, and often most humorous aspects of the English language are those colorful expressions known as *adages*, *aphorisms*, and *idioms*.

If you've traveled anywhere in the English-speaking world, you've no doubt heard someone use the phrase, "pay through the nose" or "you're just talkin' outta your ass!" Or perhaps you've been told that so-and-so had "shit a brick!" But, what do these frequently-repeated expressions actually mean?

After traveling the world for many years, inviting people to relate what they believe are the origins of these and other expressions, I've discovered that in most cases there are actually specific events thought to have spurred particular expressions. Those that have a special place in the annals of world linguistic history.

(For) all the tea in China:

Although the centuries-old bad blood between Scotland and England is pretty much a thing of the past, this long-standing rivalry is no better illustrated than in the story of the Tetley Brothers of England and the Lipton family of Scotland, that were it not for the long-standing historic contempt and distrust that existed between these countrymen, the *Tetley Tea Company* would be the biggest tea distributing company in the world instead of the second biggest. And the *Lipton Company* may not existence at all.

As the story goes, in the early 1880's, Brothers Tetley, Joseph and Edward, were successful salt dealers in England. At this same time, Sir Thomas Lipton I, who had the only tea importing company in Scotland, wanted to sell his company and immigrate to the United States. But with money scarce in Scotland at this time, he decided to try his luck in England, approaching the wealthy Lipton Brothers to buy him out.

While brother Edward was quite keen on the idea, the more loyalist brother Joseph's hatred of all things Scottish compelled him to reply, "Not for all the tea in China!" So, the deal was never made and Lipton invariably stayed in Scotland.

Little could Edward have imagined, however, that not only would *Lipton Tea* go on to become the largest tea importer in the world in the hands of Thomas Lipton II, a few years later he and his brother would also buy into the tea market, acquiring the rights to *all the tea in China*, while the Tetleys have since been limited to what is grown in India!

THE BOOK OF ADAGES, APHORISMS, IDIOMS, AND COLORFUL EXPRESSIONS

(I have) an axe to grind:

Until very recent times, even young children of America knew the dark and chilling tale of Lizzie Borden, the Massachusetts spinster accused of killing her father and stepmother with an axe in 1860.

In fact, a popular but rather ghoulish jump rope rhyme kids frequently recited was, "Lizzie Borden took an axe and gave her mother forty whacks. When she saw what she had done, she gave her father forty-one."

And although jump-roping, as well as Lizzie's condemning rhyme, have both fallen our of popularity, most adults know that Lizzie was ultimately arrested, tried, and found innocent of the charges. But almost lost to history is what followed next.

After her acquittal, Lizzie used her new-found celebrity to garner attention, and indeed, became quite the social butterfly around Falls River.

In fact, not only was the stigma of having killed her parents no stigma at all (with most people apparently believing she had actually done it), it grew into a sort of social *cache*, her dirty deeds becoming a popular topic for grade schoolers' essays, the subject of parlor games like charades, and even led to a number of socially-relevant euphemisms such as the adage, "I have an axe to grind with you."

Used much as the phrase, "I've got a bone to pick with you" is used today, an 'axe to grind' indicated that someone was angry enough to take an axe to them. And while no documented cases of violence related to this popular expression made the history books, the phrase nonetheless survived the decades and remains in our lexicon of slang a century and a half later.

Even so, it might be wise to give it more than passing consideration if this expression is directed at you. After all, look how it ended for the Bordens!

Call a spade a spade:

Long before the name Deere was associated with one of the world's largest agricultural and construction equipment manufacturing companies, the Deere family were poor dirt farmers struggling just to keep food on the table, in Vermont and later Illinois.

By the turn of the 19th century, most of the younger Deeres had given up farming and moved to Chicago, the "big city," to seek their fame and fortunes. Finally, only young John Deere was left to pick up and carry the torch of the family farm.

John, however, as the story goes, showed no aptitude whatsoever for farming, preferring instead to spend his time tending the plow mules, and was said to have been so incompetent at farming that he hadn't even picked up the common farming terminology. He usually referred to shovels and spades as "those digging *thingies*."

While his father had for many years practiced tolerance, believing that eventually his son would come around to the family tradition, a breaking point was reached one hot summer day when the elder Deere asked his son to hand him a spade

THE BOOK OF ADAGES, APHORISMS, IDIOMS, AND COLORFUL EXPRESSIONS

and received the usual query, "You mean the pointed digging thingy?" to which his father exclaimed, "*Damn* it, John, call a spade a *spade*!" It was on this crucial day that both father and son knew that John would never be a farmer.

Fortunately for the Deere clan, however, John turned out to be a much better blacksmith than farmer and subsequently gave up the family farming business shortly after his father's death.

The rest, of course, is pure Americana!

Couch potato:

While the term "couch potato" has been adopted in modern parlance to refer to someone who spends far too much time sitting on the couch—usually watching TV and eating junk food—I discovered that this expression originally referred to an experiment conducted in 1947 by one Dr. Margaret Woot, a world-renown geneticist and pioneer in gene splicing.

According to the doctor's own journal entries, Woot, a gifted but eccentric graduate of University Vienna, had set out to see if anything would grow in the dust and lint that collected in the cracks of her davenport. And far beyond her wildest expectations, she actually succeeded in growing a potato-like mutant vegetable! But then, as her journal notes explain, the experiment went terribly awry.

Apparently, the ravenous spud quickly grew to enormous proportions, finally devouring Woot and all her lab animals before being caught and dissected—or *diced*—as the case may be.

(An interesting historical side-bar is that the now world-famous kids' toy *Mr. Potato Head* was actually modeled after Woot's hideous creation!)

Dig your own grave:

When the Black Death struck Europe during the mid-14th century, the economy sustained an horrific blow. Obviously, those who fell to the plague are to be pitied for the horrendous agony they no doubt endured from the moment they contracted the deadly disease, but by comparison, many of those left behind suffered far more dire consequences.

The water became undrinkable, food became scarce, looting and pillaging became commonplace, and to make matters worse, surviving family members were held legally responsible for disposing of their dead relatives' infected bodies.

Then, as the death toll rose, taxes skyrocketed and thousands of families lost their property as one by one they were stricken, with surviving family members forced to use their last shilling to pay for a proper burial.

Capitalizing on this miserable state of affairs (there are, of course, always those anxious to benefit from the misfortune of others), many who found themselves immune to the deadly virus went in the "corpse disposal business," contracting to be paid in advance for removing the putrid bodies before they decomposed. Subsequently, many lords and wealthy land owners chose to contract in advance for their disposal rather than leave the burden to family members after they'd died.

THE BOOK OF ADAGES, APHORISMS, IDIOMS, AND COLORFUL EXPRESSIONS

But as the death toll reached astounding numbers, there simply weren't enough of the healthy to handle all the dead, so the healthy further capitalized on the wealthy by requiring the dying to dig their own graves in advance while they were still physically able.

It became common for such business transactions to go something like: "I'm in need of your services, sir. How much are you asking to move my body to the grave?"

The body-collector would ask, "You dig your own grave?"

"Yes, I'll see to it that my grave is dug."

"Very well then, six pence, three." At which time money would change hands.

(A) *dollar to a donut:*

A popular saying of the 1950s and 60s but still heard across America today, this whimsical little phrase actually dates back to 1936 and the famous *Best-Out-of-Three-Falls* wrestling match between Betty Crocker and Aunt Jemima held at Beaux-Arts Station, the predecessor of Madison Square Garden in New York City.

As the story goes, while both women were fledgling bakers vying for public notoriety, Betty repeatedly laid claim to "Aunt" Jean Jemima's secret family baking recipes. Not one to take a family affront lightly, Jean challenged Betty to a *winner-take-all* wrestling match—for all the fame, fortune, and perks that go with it—the loser quietly packing up her muffin tins and moving to parts unknown. (Wait for it…) Quite naturally, the betting line at the sounding of the first round bell was "A dollar to a donut!"

Luckily for the American public, the match ended in a draw and both women went on to find their individual niches in the highly competitive world of cookbook authoring and pancake batter making!

Don't look a gift horse in the mouth:

In modern times this quaint expression has come to mean that one shouldn't question the value of a gift; that one should graciously accept a present without first evaluating it. And while this sentiment is certainly thoughtful wisdom to live by, this does not reflect the historic origin of this phrase.

As ancient Chinese tradition explains, among the Mongols of the 6th century CE, horses were valued more than any other possession. Often more than sons or daughters, and always more than wives.

The buying and trading of horses was a major aspect of Mongol day-to-day life, and was directly equated with prestige and power. As such, horses became part of the Mongol justice system, with debts and reckoning often settled in horses.

But, since Mongols hated nothing more than having to part with their steeds—under *any* circumstance—owners would teach their animals to bite the hands of anyone other than themselves who might approach them. Thus, when required by tribal law to give up a horse in payment, should the recipient be foolish enough to check the horse's teeth (which was customary when buying a horse), the animal would abruptly clamp down on the new owner's fingers, often taking off several if not all their digits!

This would, of course, bring great joy to the one losing his horse, but great rage from the one acquiring it!

Eventually, Mongols wised up and stopped "looking gift horses in the mouth." (We won't go into detail as to what horses were trained to do should the new owner check the horse's flanks!)

(An) eye for an eye:

While many people are aware that "an eye for an eye" is part of the ancient justice system common to the Near East and western Asia, whereby the punishment for causing someone to lose an eye was having to forfeit an eye yourself, (and similarly, a hand for a hand and a leg for a leg), what is lesser known is that it was this system of evenhandedness that eventually led to the tradition of choosing arbiters (judges) to make rulings about appropriate punishment.

For example, while losing an eye for having taken an eye seemed only fair, it became a question of equitable payment when, by comparison, one of the parties was blind or had already lost one eye. Was the taking of an eye still fair when it left a man blind or had no consequence at all?

Or when the offense was the taking of a hand by someone who was already missing an arm, was it fair to then remove his only functional appendage?

Or in the case of maiming a man's servant, did it matter that the servant was old and had very few productive years left—rather than one who was young and virile?

Thus, "an eye for an eye" led to the modern system of jurisprudence whereby subjective values had to be placed on persons and possessions.

(Imagine, of course, the complications involved in assigning fair payment when the offense was slicing off a man's manhood!)

Park your carcass:

Although most Americans think of Henry Ford when thinking of the first American-made automobiles, it was actually Random E. Olds who first produced cars in the US, starting 1897.

Originally located in Lansing, Michigan, *Oldsmobile Motor Works* was moved to Detroit two years later, producing a fantastic 425 autos a year by 1901, making the *Oldsmobile* the top-selling automobile for its first few years in production. But the phrase "park your carcass" may have played a major part in that popularity!

While toying with names for his motorized vehicle, Olds considered several, but fancied one in particular: the combining of the Middle English word for "cart," *carre*, and the Old French word for "chariot," *karros*, forming what he thought was a clever and alluring description of his new motorized conveyance, the "carre-karros" or *Carkaros*. And he was just about to attach that label to his vehicles when he met with a group of prospective buyers interested in transporting several dozen models to California to open the country's first automobile distributorship.

Having simply written the name he intended to use on a sheet of paper, Olds proudly presented it to one of the buyers to see his initial reaction—but certainly didn't get what he'd expected! Mouthing the name on the paper, the man looked up at Olds in astonishment, saying, "Mr. Olds! No matter how you spell it, is still says *old dead animal*! Nobody's gonna wanna drive an Old *Carcass*! Imagine saying, 'Where should I park my Old *Carcass*?'"

Quickly seeing the short-comings of his idea, Random responded, "Very well gentlemen. Then we'll just call it the *Olds-Mobile!*" The rest, of course, is automotive history!
(But just imagine if the original name had stuck!)

Pitching woo:

While many attach a warm and fuzzy connotation to the term "pitching woo," believing it a sweet remnant of Europe's Romantic Era of the 17th and 18th centuries, historic evidence indicates that the reference is actually related to several centuries earlier and Marco Polo's historic meeting with the infamous scourge, Kublai Khan, during his historic 13th century visit to Mongolia.

As the story goes, the pompous and arrogant Polo was bent on proving his superiority to the intimidating war lord, so he challenged Khan to a show of physical strength, a game he called "pitching Woo." Woo was Khan's fiercest warrior, and said to weigh-in at well over 400 lbs!

While history does not record who won this historic meeting of brains and brawn, many believe it subsequently led to another popular expression, "Don't go getting your balls in a tangle!" (Sounds reasonable!)

Pull out all the stops:

A virtual unknown to the world of 18th century classical music until he created the famously dark and haunting masterpiece, *Toccata and Fugue in D minor*, Johann Sebastian Bach was hence deemed a genius of organ repertoire for creating the ominous organ tone behind this great work of art.

While a wide variety of organ tones were in popular use in pipe organ composition during this era (which utilized a system of various "stop" levers mounted on the keyboard), no one up to that time had discovered the ominous sound Bach had. This discovery literally made his a household name throughout Europe, and launched a career placing him among the greatest classical composers of all time.

Years later, when an eager writer (himself an aspiring musician) was penning the great maestro's biography, the writer took the opportunity to ask the aging Bach what every musician had wanted to know for nearly half a century, "How

THE BOOK OF ADAGES, APHORISMS, IDIOMS, AND COLORFUL EXPRESSIONS

did you come up with such a new and exciting sound?" No longer having a reputation to protect, Bach confided: "Hell if I know! I just pulled out all the stops!"

The phrase, of course, has taken on a somewhat different meaning in modern times!

Royal pain in the ass:

As royal Spanish court documents confirm, this dubious moniker was actually the first official title bestowed upon the famously inept explorer Christopher Columbus by Queen Isabella of Spain, after his forty-ninth failed attempt to even navigate his way out of the Straight of Gibraltar and into the Atlantic Ocean. (It was, in fact, the only honor ever bestowed upon this famously incompetent wanna-be sailor in his lifetime!)

Fed up with Columbus' repeated blunders, one can almost see Queen Isabella rolling her eyes as Columbus was again announced in the Royal Court: "His Royal Pain in the Ass... Christopher Columbus!"

(Don't go) shootin' your mouth off:

While strictly a figure of speech today, referring to someone saying far more than they should on a subject, "shooting one's mouth off" became an historic reality all across America soon after the invention of the muzzle-loaded rifle.

While muzzle-loaded pistols could easily be loaded with the barrel pointed away, the length of rifles virtually demanded that the gun be rested on the butt, pointed toward the loader, while the barrel was loaded and tamped.

While noses, eyes, ears, and, of course, fingers were also common casualties of the dangerous loading process, for some reason, mouths were the only body part preserved in common lingo!

Splitting hairs:

In many parts of America today this idiom is used to indicate that someone has taken a point of contention and argued it beyond reason; to quibble about petty distinctions.

American history, however, shows that this expression originally referred to splitting *hares* not *hairs*—relating to times of both feast and famine; and in both situations, relating to the settlement at Jamestown.

While many assume that cattle, pigs, or even chickens were the first livestock raised in America, it was actually rabbits. Or to be more precise, wild *hare*.

As surviving journal entries show, what livestock that did survive the harrowing journey across the Atlantic—which were few—proved sickly and unproductive, and died shortly after arrival, leaving the settlers without a viable source of meat.

Since most of the colonists were aspiring businessmen and not hunters, they hit upon the idea to raise hare, both for food and for trade with the local native tribes.

THE BOOK OF ADAGES, APHORISMS, IDIOMS, AND COLORFUL EXPRESSIONS

The raising of hare, however, was a double-edge sword for the settlers: If they allowed the rabbits to breed freely, they would, of course, have plenty of food and fur. If they *did* allow them to breed freely, however, a point would be reached when the number of rabbits would exceed what the settlers could care for and feed—a tricky balancing act, especially during the long winter months. Thus, "splitting," or separating hares by sex became a method of population control. But, there's more to the story.

Until this successful balance was achieved, several winters passed during which the settlers didn't have enough hare meat to go around and had to "split" hares at meal time. This meant that while a family once had the luxury of sharing a whole hare for dinner, they were forced to ration their meat, having to settle for half, or a "split" hare.

(This makes a lot more sense than splitting a human hair, now doesn't it!?)

Stop trying to make a monkey out of me:

One of the more recent additions to American vernacular, "Stop trying to make a monkey out of me" is unique in that is was not first uttered by a human, but an ape—in a manner of speaking.

In the 1960s, after several failed scientific projects aimed at teaching apes to speak, Allen and Beatrix Gardner endeavored to teach an ape American Sign Language (ASL), their first candidate being a two-year-old chimpanzee named Washoe.

So successful was Washoe at learning American Sign, however, that after learning a documented 350 words, he then developed the ability to convey his own abstract thoughts, even creating his own phrases like "metal cup drink" for *thermos*.

Having spent most of his life in the company of humans, Washoe quite naturally began taking on human behaviors as well, seeming to think of himself as human—insisting on eating, watching TV, and dressing like a human.

The extent of his cross-species transformation became quite apparent when one day Beatrix asked Washoe to peel and eat a banana, at which time he gave what Beatrix described as 'an indignant facial expression' and signed, "No make monkey me!"

Washoe then smoothed his smoking jacket, poured himself a stiff brandy, and lit up a Turkish cigarette!

That hit the spot:

A popular colloquialism used today to mean that a drink or meal has satiated a particular thirst or hunger, the "spot" this adage originally referred to is actually of a much different nature, as history of the American Old West shows.

While many of the eminent gunslingers of the Old West have taken a prominent place in popular lore as the greatest marksmen of all time—Billy the Kid, Wild Bill Hickok, and John Wesley Harden among them—legend confirms that Annie Oakley was actually the greatest shot of all time. But without

THE BOOK OF ADAGES, APHORISMS, IDIOMS, AND COLORFUL EXPRESSIONS

the occurrence of one specific event, this fact may have been forever lost to the past.

Despite her known prowess with a six-shooter around the prairie towns, being a woman meant that reputation alone wasn't enough to land her a job with Buffalo Bill's traveling *Wild West Show*. Forced to first demonstrate her shooting skills, Bill told her that if she could hit a playing card with a single shot at 75 yards at full gallop, she could join his show.

As history confirms, not only did Annie hit the card at full gallop, she plugged the ace of spades dead center, to which one of the other performers exclaimed, "She hit the center! She actually hit the *spot!*" to which Annie allegedly replied, "Damn right! Care to risk your manhoods, gentlemen?"

Little Annie Oakley not only went on to become the headliner of *Bill's Wild West Show*, she became American's first recognized female celebrity and the highest paid woman in the Western Hemisphere!

Turn coat:

While this adage has come to denote someone who has abandoned loyalties and switched to the opposing side, the true origin of this term is much more literal, and involves the turning of a coat inside out so as not to be identified as part of either side.

The oldest documented occurrence of this behavior is attributed to one Thomas Woolworth, who in the fall of 1862, had gotten separated from his Confederate unit in South

Carolina, and found himself on the wrong side of the Mason-Dixon Line.

Wishing to live to fight another day, Corporal Woolworth decided to remove the collar from his grey wool jacket, turn it inside out, and then discard his slouch hat and long-barrel in the bushes. Filling his haversack with apples from a near-by orchard, he casually munched on a Granny Smith as he strolled past Union soldiers virtually unnoticed, eventually making his way back to his unit.

But this story ultimately does not end well.

So as not to set a precedent, Corporal Woolworth was summarily executed by firing squad a short time later for desecration of government property and surrendering his weapon to the enemy!

Who knew that feigning neutrality was such a serious crime!

Whole nine yards:

The story of Betsy Ross and the making of the first official flag of the United States is, of course, known even to young school children. Indeed, an eternal debt of gratitude is owed this remarkable woman who created what is probably the most important piece of seamstress work in American history.

But what is lesser known is the back-story of this patriotic tale, and the scandal the making of Old Glory involved by the time of its completion.

THE BOOK OF ADAGES, APHORISMS, IDIOMS, AND COLORFUL EXPRESSIONS

According to diaries of the time, among 18th century Philadelphian society, Betsy Ross was considered a pretentious elitist prone to arrogance, snobbery, and one-upmanship. Frequently boasting of her family heritage, expensive imported possessions, and important society acquaintances, she succeeded in effectively ostracizing herself, becoming a renowned outsider among the women of Philadelphia.

Soon, rumors began to spread that Betsy was a wanton trollop who used her seamstress skills to lure soldiers to her bed, using the pretense of making them woolen undergarments to wear into the battlefield.

And so it was amidst this social tension that the snooty seamstress was charged by General Washington with this most prestigious mission, and then proceeded to cause a stir of historic proportions the day she entered the only fabric shop in Philadelphia and placed three bolts of cloth on the counter:

"I'll take three yards of the blue and six of the red," several of Philadelphia's upper-crust over-heard her say.

"And, the white?" the shop owner asked.

After a pregnant pause Betsy picked up the bolt and said haughtily, "Why, I'll take the whole nine yards!"

The shop erupted.

"Whole nine yards?!" one lady said, fanning herself.

"Is that really what she said?" uttered another. "Why, that supercilious elitist! Imagine! She's probably making night shirts for all her night *guests*!"

They, of course, had no idea what her true mission was. Still, the expression has survived the ages—as well as the flag she made!

(A) *wink is as good as a nod to a blind horse:*

As reflected by 16th century Church documents, by the time the famous genius Michelangelo had reached the ripe old age of eighty, friends and colleagues had begun to suspect that he'd lost touch with reality.

He'd began ignoring even the most basic grooming habits, rarely bathing, seldom changing clothes, and most disturbingly, had started sleeping in full regalia, including shoes. His personal assistant is quoted as once confiding, "He has sometimes gone so long without taking his shoes off that then the skin came away, like a snake's, with the boots."

Adding to this, he rarely spoke to others, and when he did, had a tendency to end conversations by simply walking away in mid-sentence.

Suspicions were finally confirmed when upon the death of his only brother, Michelangelo insisted on skipping to the funeral chanting the nonsensical—and quite inappropriate—"A wink is as good as a nod to a blind horse! A wink is as good as a nod to a blind horse! A wink is as good as a nod to a blind horse!"

THE BOOK OF ADAGES, APHORISMS, IDIOMS, AND COLORFUL EXPRESSIONS

After this incident, Michelangelo spent his remaining years locked in his studio for his own protection!

You're just talkin' outta your ass:

Though variations of this highly visual expression can be heard in cultural settings all over the world, its origin can actually be traced to 550 BCE Mesopotamia and a local desert grifter named Ishmael, who unwittingly became the world's first ventriloquist when a skeptical onlooker exposed his "Bathsheba the Talking Mule" routine.

Subsequently, as oral tradition explains, Ishmael became the inspiration for a whole string of aspiring Mid-Eastern entertainers seeking to share the voice-thrower's limelight (or sunlight, as the case may be).

And if we can trust oral tradition—which we always do—Ishmael then went on to establish the first talent agency in history, becoming the world's first theatrical agent! And of course today, Hollywood circles are full of people who consistently 'talk outta their asses'!

CHAPTER TWO:
"Myths & Urban Legends"

Myths and urban legends are fundamental aspects of every known society in the world.

Myths become the foundation of a culture's belief system, while urban legends serve to explain the unanswerable oddities that arise in everyday life. Between the two, the origins of many commonly used adages and expressions can be traced.

But by and large, it's often impossible to distinguish myth and urban legend from pure malarkey!

THE BOOK OF ADAGES, APHORISMS, IDIOMS, AND COLORFUL EXPRESSIONS

Animal magnetism:

According to the Japanese creation myth, after creating the earth, seas, and clouds, the god of all creation was bored and lonely so he created two lesser gods, Izanagi and Izanami.

He placed the two new gods on the land and told them to start creating animals to inhabit the earth, and that he would periodically visit the earth from his place in the heavens to share their company and check on their progress.

Izanami, the more intelligent of the two new gods, immediately set out to create the most harmonious animals she could think of and soon filled the earth with rabbits, songbirds, deer, unicorns, and all sorts of beautiful creatures that quickly multiplied and spread to the far corners of the earth.

Izanagi, however, the much less intelligent of the two new gods, created the most fierce animals he could think of, making boars, poisonous snakes, vultures, and other horrible creatures that constantly attacked each other and quickly vanished from the face of the earth.

When the god of creation made his first visit to earth, he loved what he saw. Everywhere he looked, gentle creatures flocked and flew and multiplied.

Upon asking Izanagi which creatures he had created, the new god admitted that all he had created had died or killed one other. Disappointed but understanding, the god of creation said, "That is because you created no animal magnetism to draw them together. They must be made to be attracted to one another. Try again."

After a short visit, the god of creation returned to his place in the heavens. Izanagi and Izanami returned to their creation duties.

One day soon after, Izanami heard Izanagi calling frantically, "Izanami, please come help me! I did as the god of creation told me, but look!" As Izanami stood looking at Izanagi's new creations, she realized just how dull-witted her brother really was.

He had made his new creations truly *magnetic*, and there were now thousands of animals roaming the earth in pairs—and sometimes threes—unable to separate themselves, and tearing each other limb from limb in anger!

When the god of creation saw the stupid thing Izanagi had done, he removed all his powers to create. Izanagi became the world's first mortal. And the phrase that ruined him, remains in our vocabulary to this day!

Born with a silver spoon in their mouth:

Although this expression can be heard in any region of the United States, used to refer to someone who was born into a wealthy family and never had to make their own way in life, urban legend traces this highly demeaning phrase to the actual occurrence of this strange phenomenon at a remote hospital in East Germany around 1842.

THE BOOK OF ADAGES, APHORISMS, IDIOMS, AND COLORFUL EXPRESSIONS

While it is commonly believed that all documents relating to this event were intentionally destroyed, local folklore contends that baby "Trudy" Ledbetter, born to Gertrude and Heinrich Ledbetter of South Dessau, was indeed born with a piece of silver cutlery in her tiny mouth!

Legend describes a terribly embarrassed Mrs. Ledbetter, who would offer no explanation whatsoever for this occurrence (while blushing profusely), and an irate Mr. Ledbetter who voiced many scathing accusations—all of which "made the veins in his neck bulge out!"

The Ledbetters are said to have disappeared from Germany shortly after this scandalous event, having moved to France where they lived out their lives under assumed names!

Busy as a one-legged man at an ass-kicking contest:

This comical expression is said to have actually originated in the time of the first Olympiad Games, which in its early inception featured several unusual competitions common for the times.

Events such as the *one-legged-ass-kicking* contest, the *who-can-stuff-the-most-olives-in-their-nose* competition, and the *boulder-catching* event were met with considerable trepidation and skepticism, and of course, resulted in substantial injuries.

Fortunately for today's Olympiads, these events were eventually replaced by the stade race, Greco-Roman wrestling, and the far less dangerous, shot put!

Don't air your dirty laundry:

This old Gypsy proverb has been passed down through the generations for longer than any Gypsy can remember, but is believed to date back to the first Gypsies to leave India.

Said to have the keenest sense of smell of any people, Gypsies live by the code that if you leave your dirty laundry to air-out—as is the custom with many wandering people—your enemies will catch wind of your presence and follow the scent!

Said to have the olfactory capacity to do this themselves, Gypsy traditional stories are filled with cautionary tales of those who have ignored this warning and fallen prey to enemies and outsiders who have caught wind of their garments and were then able to sneak up on them in the darkness of the night.

Likened to bloodhounds, Gypsies profess to be able to distinguish not only a Gypsy from members of others cultures, but distinguish individual tribes—just by the laundry they air!

Don't be such a nit-picker:

Unlikely as it may seem, this somewhat disturbing expression probably derived from an actual occupation held by many peasants during the Dark Ages of Europe to supplement what they earned as peasant dirt farmers.

With water scarce and plumbing as yet unknown in this place and time, it's widely believed that "nit picking" was one of several fairly well-paid services one could provide wealthy land owners!

THE BOOK OF ADAGES, APHORISMS, IDIOMS, AND COLORFUL EXPRESSIONS

"Crud scrapers" and "dust blowers," however, are said to have been better paid for their dubious services—requiring a bit more finesse!

Drunk as a skunk:

This odoriferous little saying seems to have originated with one Arlo "Shaky" Polk, and his pet skunk, Smelly Lester, both of Black Bottom Hollow, West Virginia.

As the story goes, even though "Shaky" already had the most successful corn *squeezin's* business in all the hollow, old Shaky got it in his head that he could get rich faster if he offered folks a double-or-nothing deal whereby if they could out-drink Smelly Lester, they could get a jug for free.

What's important to know is that Smelly Lester wasn't your ordinary woods-dwelling skunk, but was raised by Shaky since he was a pup, and nursed on Shaky's corn squeezings. In fact, Lester was Shaky's official taste tester after Shaky's taste buds burned off from tasting one batch of whisky too many!

As the story goes, with Smelly Lester's near-immunity to corn whisky, the old skunk proceeded to drink the first 20 customers under the table, after which no one would take Shaky up on his deal.

Even so, Smelly Lester had set a precedent. From then on in Black Bottom Hollow, if you weren't "Lester the Skunk drunk," you weren't drunk at all!

"Drunk as a skunk" was what every Hillbilly aspired to achieve!

Hair of the dog:

Of no real surprise, I've been able to uncover numerous oral accounts from many parts of the world that attribute this expression (that typically refers to the idea that the best cure for a hangover is more of the same) to ancient curatives which actually contained dog hair!

Thought to possess unique curative powers, potion-makers and shaman of many cultures believe that particular feathers, fur, scales, nails, and hair have the ability to cure a number of ailments.

But as regards hangover cures, it seems that not just any old dog hair will work. It's gotta be the hair of the legendary "booze hound"!

Hind sight:

While the hideous and shocking results of the H. G. Wells character Dr. Moreau are restricted to the written page and silver screen, urban legend says that this never-taken-literally expression actually relates to the real-life experiments of one "Dr." Hobart Griffin, an early 20th century mortician who decided to follow in the fictional character's footsteps and attempt to create human-animal hybrids.

Known to have idolized H. G. Wells, and believing the great science-fiction writer was covertly advocating the creation of a race of cross-bred mutants, "Dr" Griffin conducted his own gruesome experiments, utilizing human body parts pilfered from the morgue and animal parts from neighborhood strays, and actually succeeded in grafting a Great Dane's paw in place of his own hand!

By the time this madman was discovered in the basement laboratory of his Boston brownstone in historic Beacon Hill, he had also succeeded in creating a mutant half-cat, half-rabbit creature with an ocular ability requiring it to walk backwards, directed by its rear-end!

Bostonians say Griffin's hideous creations can still be seen in large glass jars of embalming fluid at Harvard Medical School!

(You couldn't) hit a bear in the ass with a bass fiddle:

Said to be the oldest known version of the now-popular children's birthday game, *pin the tail on the donkey*, "hit a bear in the ass with a bass fiddle" was a favorite with children of the Ozarks for at least a century before Federal authorities caught on.

After encountering hundreds of bears with hairless backsides who became horribly violent just by the sound of the bass fiddle, an investigation showed generations of mountain kids missing various limbs, but who could run faster than jackrabbits!

Hop, skip, and a jump:

It probably doesn't occur to many of us today, but how did our prehistoric ancestors compute distance before the invention of standardized linear measurement?

Before feet, yards, and miles were conceived, how far was it across a commonly-used field? Or village to village? Or to the edge of *no return*?

Well, as common cross-cultural legends explain, ancient man used the most logical measurements available to him, the length of body parts, the space covered by an average hop, or the distance a man could typically walk in a day.

And while even today in some remote parts of the world such as Australia's Outback and Africa's Sahara region we can still hear a phrase like, "It's two-days' walk from here," standardized linear measurement has made it unnecessary to say, "It's twenty hops and a jump down to the river bed." Or, "Just fifty skips straight ahead to the apple tree."

But 50,000 years ago, what choice did they have?

Keep an eye out:

In the ancient Orient, robbers and thieves became as much a part of the spice trade as the legitimate buyers and traders who transported pepper, nutmeg, cinnamon, coriander, cumin, and mace along the caravan trail.

But far from limiting their looting to spices, brigands would steal anything of value from those foolish enough not to travel in large caravans—which is why caravans were formed. They were infamous for taking anything of value from jewelry to silken clothing, shoes to gold teeth, when desperate enough.

THE BOOK OF ADAGES, APHORISMS, IDIOMS, AND COLORFUL EXPRESSIONS

Since retribution in this part of the world commonly involved the slicing off of a hand or an ear—or even the popping out an eye—the wearing of prosthetic limbs and glass eyes became common occurrences. As such, these artificial body parts became part of those things highly valued and frequently purloined along the route.

Many thieves, however, had reputations for having a sense of honor, known to look upon the lame with a degree of pity. Thus, caravan traders would routinely remove and stow away artificial body parts such as hook hands and glass eyes, hoping to play on thieves' sense of pity.

Thus, "keep an eye out" was a common phrase meaning to appear half blind so that thieves would see you as less of a target and *hopefully* take pity on you!

(Take a) long walk off a short pier:

Used the world over in one variation or another, this little idiom is believed to have originally been part of the dubious legacy of none other than the suave and debonair Frenchman "Savage Sam," the only known sea-sick pirate of the Seven Seas.

Because of his fear of water, Savage Sam was forced to devise this version of "Walk the Plank" for all the ship captains and crews he scourged dock-side—which of course, weren't many.

(Sam, of course, had no ship or buccaneers, but that didn't seem to deter his resolve to pillage!)

Low man on the totem pole:

As Native American oral tradition tells it, a little known fact of Pacific Northwest Indian history (and one that embarrasses Native Americans of the region to this day), is that before it occurred to anyone that physical likenesses could be carved from red cedar logs, totem poles were erected using living tribesmen.

(Living animals were also attempted—but, of course, they were having none of that!)

Forced to remain stacked head-to-foot from sunrise to sunset, the totem tribesman on top typically had the hardest time remaining perfectly still in the errant breeze, while the low man on the pole had the miserable job of supporting all the weight.

This tradition continued for more than a century until a canoe builder of the Manakata people conceived of the idea of carving a wooden totem pole to honor those of the living totem tradition.

Considered a stroke of genius, subsequent totems represented many of the early pole-standers who were later revered as living gods for their endurance and super-human feats of strength!

THE BOOK OF ADAGES, APHORISMS, IDIOMS, AND COLORFUL EXPRESSIONS

Nose to the grindstone:

This colorful colloquialism, which can still be heard in everyday conversation throughout the Eastern and mid-West US today, is widely attributed to a well-known miller named Jonah J. Johnson of Garden City, Kansas, whose flour was once the hands-down favorite of bakers for hundreds of miles around.

In fact, Johnson was so successful that he was just about to open flour shops in several neighboring counties.

Everything changed, however, one spring day when neighbor Jane Smith accidentally witnessed the disturbing truth about how Johnson got that special, "down-home" taste!

(In retrospect, everyone said they should have been suspicious that Johnson always had a scab on his nose!)

Pay through the nose:

As urban legend goes, this colorful phrase is most often attributed to a now extinct Inuit tribe of Alaska who after discovering the quaint pleasantry of rubbing noses, attempted to initiate several other "nose" customs as well.

Fortunately for all involved, drinking through the nose, whistling through the nose, and talking through the nose never really caught on either!

(It's) raining cats and dogs:

A common urban legend of the US Midwest, this weather phenomenon is said to actually be a rather common occurrence in America's "tornado alley," where chickens, fish, rabbits, snakes, and yes, even cats and dogs have been known to be picked up in twisters and then "rained" on unsuspecting residents miles away—minutes or even hours later!

Perhaps more shocking, however, are the accounts of horses, goats, and, yes—even *cows*—that have dropped from the sky and caused serious destruction to life and limb as was the well-known case involving one Dottie Trueheart of Kansas.

As Kansans tell it, a cow from the next county actually dropped through the roof of the Trueheart farm house, killing Dottie dead in her bed. Making this tale even more disturbing is that at the time, Dottie was there with a man not her husband—who was also crushed to death under the massive weight.

Ever since that occurrence, cows of western Kansas have been revered as harbingers of divine retribution and treated like supernatural messengers, getting to roam freely about the countryside!

Shit a brick:

After several years of tracking the origin of this difficult to imagine expression, I was finally able to trace it to a very talented Silkie rooster that once lived in China during the Manchu Dynasty, under the rule of Emperor Kangxi.

THE BOOK OF ADAGES, APHORISMS, IDIOMS, AND COLORFUL EXPRESSIONS

As Chinese legend explains it, for most of its life, this famous rooster known as Wudi had lived in the lap of luxury due to possessing the remarkable ability to produce brick-shaped droppings. Apparently, several additions to the Royal Palace had been made possible due to his amazing talent!

Unfortunately, as Chinese legend further explains, a dark day arrived when the fat and aging rooster, while apparently constipated, was then upstaged by the discovery of a young Mongolian goose that could do one better—lay golden eggs!

(With China's renowned love of orange-glazed goose, there's no need to tell you how that story ended!)

But it seems only fitting to give Wudi a nod of respect whenever we hear the expression "shit a brick" used!

Take it with a grain of salt:

Although I haven't been able to pinpoint its specific origin, several sources agree that this seemingly figurative expression is actually rooted in ancient superstition of the Orient from a time when salt was believed to possess magical qualities.

Used as a food preservative for thousands of years, the science behind why it kept meat and other foods from spoiling remained unknown until recent decades, and was long assumed to involve magic.

Salt itself was believed to possess properties far beyond the purely practical.

Thus, for centuries it was common practice to *take* a grain of salt with natural curatives when black magic was suspected. Likewise, it was added to a cup of water or milk when the source was thought to be cursed. And believe it or not, a grain of salt was even placed inside the vagina of a woman of questionable virtue before bedding her, lest one's manhood should shrivel up and fall off!

Talking Gibberish:

The fantastic city of Gibber is said to have once existed in central Arabia, about one hundred and fifty miles east of the ancient city of Medina.

Once a mere oasis along the busy camel caravan route between Egypt and China, over the period of a century it became a thriving and bustling city where trade took place 24 hours a day, 365 days a year, with merchants coming from as far away as Mongolia, India, and Britain.

Out of this mix of customs and languages grew a *pidgin* form of communication comprised of elements of a dozen different languages, becoming what language experts call a *lingua franca;* a common language of trade and commerce. And while certain terms and phrases from this hybrid language can still be heard in modern Turkish, Iranian, and Hindi languages, the Gibberish language ceased to exist once Gibber returned to the sand from where it rose.

Now a dead language, linguists are hoping to discover ancient sources to revive this language said to be a lyrical, sing-song language, more beautiful than any spoken today!

THE BOOK OF ADAGES, APHORISMS, IDIOMS, AND COLORFUL EXPRESSIONS

Two left feet:

While this expression is often used to describe someone who is clumsy and dances *as if* they had two left feet, in several parts of the US, urban legends abound about individuals who were actually born with two left feet!

In Memphis, Tennessee, for example, there's the legend of "Left Feet Larry," a guitarist who had one of the most skilled pair of hands ever to play the blues, but had to put both legs in one pant leg when he performed to keep his feet from tapping two different rhythms!

And then there's Laverne "Lefty" Goodleaf of Saginaw, Michigan, known for getting around town on a bicycle she rode side-saddle with both feet on one pedal so she could keep from riding in continuous circles! (Rumor says she rode out of town one day and just never came back.)

But perhaps the most interesting character was a man who called himself "Leapin' Leonard," who apparently succeeded in starting a catchy little dance craze called the *Left Leg Leap* back in 1958 in Spokane, Washington.

While few current Spokane residents can remember much about the dance itself, I was able to locate a photo of Leonard demonstrating his signature "leap" at a high school dance, in the school's yearbook the *Tamarack*. And from what I could tell, it would appear that Leonard may have indeed been on his way to phenomenal success if he hadn't made one fatal mistake.

Apparently responding to a suggestion from the crowd to "put your best foot forward!" Leonard became momentarily confused, his feet became entangled, and he fell from the bandstand, breaking his back in seven places! People say Leonard never walked again.

Sometime in the early 60s Leonard just disappeared from sight and was never heard from again—gone but certainly not forgotten!

CHAPTER THREE:

"Quaint Beginnings"

As the English language evolves, morphs, and interacts with other languages, new phrases find their way into our idiomatic vocabulary virtually everyday.

While some adages and aphorisms end-up as part of a regional linguistic package—like the use of "knee-high to a grasshopper" in Georgia or "slippery as shit" in Ohio—others seem to float free-form around the country, turning up in the most unexpected places.

Still others, that have made their way from distant lands, take on an entirely different meaning in our cultural setting than they were ever intended to.

In any regard, many have what can only be considered "quaint beginnings."

All haired-over:

One of the more fascinating aspects of culture—whether ancient or present-day—involves rites of passage and customs regarding when a society deems an individual old enough to be considered of marrying age.

In ancient Egypt, Asia, and China, for example, it was not unheard of for children as young as eight years-of-age to marry. And for a thousand years or more in many parts of Africa, South America, and Southeast Asia, arranged marriages have been consummated as early as twelve years-of-age.

Similarly, in the Jewish religion, there is a long tradition of deeming girls at age twelve and boys at age thirteen as mature and, thus, responsible for their actions. And even today in the US, a female can be wed as early as fourteen years-of-age, with parental consent.

But while many societies around the world continue to be at odds concerning when a girl should be considered "mature," the Irish settlers of Appalachia used a very simple process to determine maturity, directed by the *obvious* signs that puberty had arrived: when a girl's *nether region* was "all haired-over."

Say what you will, there would seem to be some logic to this approach!

An arm and a leg:

After tracking the origin of this dubious phrase half way around the world and back, I came to discover that "an arm and a leg" is actually "minimum wage" on Papua New Guinea, and among several other cannibalistic cultures inhabiting islands of the South Pacific off the coast of Australia!

And as it turns out, this is actually a substantial raise in pay which for over a century was merely *a hand and a foot*!

Apple of my eye:

Although the formal study of human anatomy was one of the first areas of science to be developed in the ancient world—traceable to ancient Greece, Rome, and China—various parts of the body which were initially labeled according to their believed purpose, shape, or physical appearance, continued to carry the same colloquial terminology even into modern times.

For instance, once it was discovered that the internal organs occupying the space on either sides of the hips resembled *kidney* beans, they became known by that euphemistic designation from then on—and continue to be even to this day.

Similarly, the buttocks (the bum, rump, bottom, Gluteus Maximus) was for centuries referred to as the *cussin* (cushion), the Gallic term that described the perceived purpose of these two fleshy cheeks, but a term that fell out of common use only in the past century.

And likewise, parts of the human eye were given very relatable names like "the reflection," for the *pupil*, and the "apple" for the eye *ball*, terms that remained in common use well into the late 19th century.

Even the word "iris," which today we think of as a comparison to the light-adjusting mechanism of a camera (or vice versa), derived not from photographic technology, but from the plant, which ancient man thought displays colors similar to that of the eye!

Artsy-fartsy:

The great Dutch painter Vincent van Gogh's many quirks and idiosyncrasies are, of course, nearly as famous as the artist's exquisite work itself. Fits of uncontrollable rage, bouts of indescribable confusion, and severe mood swings were just the tips of the proverbial personality iceberg.

And in that he preferred to live in slums (even when benefactors offered clean quarters), cavorted with prostitutes—and even married one—(when the finer ladies of Europe offered themselves to him), only bathed when physically forced (and often was by his brother Theo), and opted to dine night after night on butter beans and cheap wine (even when he'd received sizable advances for his work), it should be of no great surprise that the artistic genius was also one of the most gaseous and fowl smelling artists in history. The man apparently reeked!

Coined by close friend and fellow artist Paul Gauguin, who often spoke on van Gogh's behalf rather than allow well-to-do benefactors endure Vincent's incessant and unapologetic gas emissions, "artsy-fartsy," became the term Gauguin used to describe his work: half art, half fart!

THE BOOK OF ADAGES, APHORISMS, IDIOMS, AND COLORFUL EXPRESSIONS

Gauguin was once quoted as saying, "I tell you, the angst in Vincent's art has nothing to do with the bats in his belfry, only the ones that seem to have crawled up his rectum and died!"

Catch a buzz:

Despite the modern connotation relating to the achievement of a certain level of intoxication via alcohol or drugs, centuries ago the term "buzz" was simply the common term for a bumblebee.

Kids, and of course, beekeepers, typically caught *buzzes* for fun, or wholly practical purposes.

Similarly, butterflies were once called "flutter-byes," wasps were "dagger tails," houseflies were "shoos," and cock roaches, well, they appear to have always called cock roaches!

(Some creatures just don't seem to deserve fanciful monikers!)

Chew the fat:

Before the invention of chewing gum in the 1860s, most every known culture of the world had their preferred choice of natural recreational chewing material.

The ancient inhabitants of Finland, for example, started chewing birch bark tar some 5000 years ago, the ancient Greeks chewed wads of mastic tree gum, while many other cultures chose gum-like substances made from plants, resins, and various grasses.

But for many people of the tundra and Arctic Circle where such natural materials were scarce, the sinew of the seal, walrus, or deer was preferred; essentially, the *fat*.

When Inuit shaman discovered in more recent centuries that "chewing fat" actually has many dental and health benefits, it became customary among many groups to sit and "chew the fat" after a meal, during which a bowl or basket of bite-sized pieces of sinew or blubber were passed around while promoting a cordial, conversational atmosphere.

While the formal invention of chewing gum did not perpetuate the long-standing social—or health—aspects into modern times, it can still be seen promoted in many of the old magazine ads in which entire families are shown sitting around sharing a *chew*!

Don't give me no lip:

Although today "Don't give me no lip!" is a common retort heard from parents warning their kids not to sass them back, this phrase was probably first heard at an oasis caravan stop in Morocco called the *House of Sirhan* some 2000 years ago, where broiled camel tongue has been the house specialty since Biblical times.

Even today, like his ancient ancestor Sirhan I, the current chief cook and butcher, Sirhan XXXI, is known to trick unwitting customers by substituting lips, ears, tails, and other unsavory animal parts for the prized *tongue*.

THE BOOK OF ADAGES, APHORISMS, IDIOMS, AND COLORFUL EXPRESSIONS

Thus, it has long been tradition to call out, "And, don't give me no *lip!*" upon ordering, the customary way of letting Sirhan know that you're no tourist and are wise to his distasteful—albeit traditional—deceptions!

Guess what, chicken butt:

As the first-ever US Children's Poet Laureate, Jack Prelutsky has certainly made quite a name for himself with the penning of the classic kids' poem, "Last Night I Dreamed of Chickens." But as his first attempt at rhyme—"guess what, chicken butt"—clearly demonstrates, his early works were certainly nothing to get too excited about!

"We just thought he had a thing about chicken butts," his mother said candidly in a recent interview. "We didn't know he was dreaming about the damn things and that he'd get famous doing it!"

(My) hat's off to you:

Thought to have originated in the Near East among Bedouin tribes, the practice of talking off one's hat, (or turban, in the original setting), was first initiated as a custom in an effort for rival bands or tribes to establish trust when first meeting to establish alliances.

Since it had been a centuries-old custom for Arabs to keep a small knife called a *shafra* concealed in their turbans, it was considered a show of good-will to take off one's turban to reveal the blade hidden inside.

While this congenial gesture didn't mean that one no longer carried a knife in this manner, it simply meant that out of respect for one's host, you voluntarily showed where the weapon was hidden.

This custom eventually made its way to Europe via British adventurers who interacted with Bedouins throughout Arabia and Africa, and is thought to have inspired the design of the 19th century British "bowler," a hat sufficiently roomy enough to conceal a sizable weapon—the Derringer said to have been the preferred weapon of choice.

Through the centuries, "hat's off" came to denote a simple show of respect or nod of approval!

I don't want to hear a peep out of you:

As only American history buffs may be aware, until the early 1800s, it was common practice in the United States for entire families to sleep in one room.

In fact, it wasn't until the early 19th century that the idea of separate bedrooms became a practical reality in most American homes.

This meant that in addition to parents and children sharing the same sleeping quarters, families who had live-in help also had their maids and other servants sleeping in the common bedroom—most often on the floor at the foot of their masters' bed.

This ultimately meant that while parents might routinely wait for the kids to go to sleep before engaging in sex, having other adults in the room essentially meant having resident, full-time *voyeurs*!

The phrase "I don't want to hear a peer out of you" was actually late 18th century vernacular for, 'We're going to be having sex tonight, so I trust it won't be necessary for you to watch'—*"peep"* being a coy colloquialism for "watching." (Also related to calling the eyes, "peepers.")

Apparently, while Colonials were accustomed to having their marital grunts and groans being overheard, they didn't want to be observed making them!

I'll be dipped in frog shit:

One of the more difficult expressions to track down, I came to discover that this phrase is actually one of several punishment options open to the little known "choose-your-own-penalty" society of the South Pacific, the *So-Whats*.

Having never developed what would be considered a conventional crime and punishment system as in other parts of the world, this culture—which still exists today—allows offenders to choose from a list of what their society considers appropriate penalties for their misdeeds.

For example, if you fail to laugh at your neighbor's joke (whether it's funny or not), your options are laughing from the mountain top until you lose your voice, walking around all day with your fingers in your ears, or writing a musical number based on the accomplishments of the one you offended, complete with dance choreography!

Being dipped in frog shit, which, incidentally, is considered one of the harshest penalties imposed, is one possible punishment for having borrowed something and not returned it at the agreed upon time. The other options are sticking your tongue out under the noon-day sun until it's sunburned, or writing 'I will not forget to return what I borrow ever again' 1000 times in the sand.

Nit wit:

Before finding his now-famous niche in human sexuality studies at Indiana University, Dr. Alfred Kinsey (of the *Kinsey Reports*) spent most of his time studying bugs and was considered by faculty and fellow students alike to be quite flaky and likely to flunk out of school altogether.

Among his many bug-related studies were lengthy dissertations on the remarkable super-human strength of the earthworm, the admirable personality traits of the German cockroach, and the irrepressible wit and humor of the common nit!

Apparently, everything changed for Alfred once he finally lost his virginity at the age of forty-five!

THE BOOK OF ADAGES, APHORISMS, IDIOMS, AND COLORFUL EXPRESSIONS

On the cuff:

One phrase that closely matches its original meaning, the expression "on the cuff" apparently originated in the early 1800's in America's Old West.

During this pioneering era when most towns were centers for miners, cattle drivers, and local farmers to periodically pick up supplies, even the most cosmopolitan cities of the Old West were dusty and dirty places where it was common for even fine ladies and gentlemen to go about town with the bottom edges of their dresses and pant cuffs filthy from the unpaved and often muddy streets.

Even more subjected to the grime of the towns were men's shirt collars and cuffs that got so filthy that they couldn't even be scrubbed clean with lye—often ruining a shirt with just a single wearing.

Eventually, however, someone got the ingenious idea to make disposable collars and cuffs made of paper that could easily be discarded and cheaply replaced. Soon, most general stores carried boxes of paper collars and cuffs that could be purchased for about a dime.

But since men's cuffs *were* made of paper (easy to replace and cheaply so), it became a matter of practicality to use them like scratch pads for jotting down information, keeping tallies in poker games, and even sending messages.

By the mid-1800s, this habit evolved into the custom of writing IOUs for meals, supplies, or even for running a tab at the local saloon, whereby a debtor simply signed his cuff (most likely put his "x") then tore it off and presented it to his benefactor like an endorsed contract. And just like today, getting a meal or a drink "on the cuff" meant getting it now and paying for it later!

Pretty as a picture:

While this seemingly benign expression may sound self-explanatory, it would seem that a little background is called for to understand the true significance of this folksy, old phrase originating in the time of America's expansion westward.

In the early days of photography, average people didn't own photographic equipment. It was quite expensive and required formal film-processing knowledge.

Thus, photographers rarely took photos of townsfolk for free, but usually required payment even if only enough to cover the cost of film and chemicals, but often accepting services like clothes washing or free meals.

But, since subjects were paying for the photographic experience, it quickly became tradition to dress in one's Sunday best, often taking hours to prepare. Men typically got haircuts and borrowed store-bought suits, while women put on their best attire—which was usually their funeral dress! But there's more!

Wanting to give themselves the *life-like,* picture-perfect perception of beauty common to the times, the town undertaker was typically called upon to make them up with rouge, lipstick, and eyebrow pencil (men, too), paid a few pennies for his particular expertise. (Undertakers were essentially the first make-up artists!) So, by the time the shutter was finally snapped, the subjects rarely looked anything like their living selves!

Thus, looking "pretty as a picture" actually meant looking nothing like yourself, and most often like you were dressed to be laid out in a pine box to meet your maker!

Put a lid on it:

Until the mid-20th century, hats were considered an essential part of every man's wardrobe, particularly throughout Europe and the United States. And whether it was a cowboy, derby, fedora, panama, or top hat, no matter the setting, it was considered uncouth for men to speak—or even greet someone on the street—with their hat on.

This meant that when encountering someone you knew, "civilized" men quickly took off their hat before beginning a conversation or even saying a cordial "hello." And it is from this quaint custom that the phrase "put a lid on it" was born!

For example, if you were visiting a household and the host wanted to indicate that it was time for you to leave, they could simply hand you your hat, knowing that once you put it on, all conversation would cease—and there'd be no further reason to stay.

Similarly, theater-goers would throw their hats onto the stage to let performers know it was time for them to shut up and get off the stage; what they were selling was no longer wanted!

By the mid 1950's, hats had all but gone out of style in the US, but the hat "traditions" did not die easily. Since hats had colloquially become known as "lids" the decade before, the expression "put a lid on it" came to mean that someone was talking too much or too long, and it was time for them to put on their hat and leave.

Even with hats no longer in the social mix, the expression survived and can still be heard today—even by those who are too young to know what it actually refers to!

Slippery as shit:

Before the advent of commercial lubricating grease in the 19th century, various animal excrement was apparently used to grease wagon wheels and make other mechanical parts run smoother. (Pioneering towns all across the US attest to this fact.)

Far less expensive than store-bought oil, and far less valuable than animal fat, *shit*, especially that of geese, was a highly prized, quite effective lubricant. Indeed, since many of the time considered goose meat tough and unsavory, most who raised geese did so for the supply of *grease* they produced!

Thus, in later years after the invention of commercial lubricants, there was no greater endorsement for a product than to be touted as "slippery as shit!" Some early manufacturers even printed that directly on the label!

THE BOOK OF ADAGES, APHORISMS, IDIOMS, AND COLORFUL EXPRESSIONS

(Give me the) straight poop:

The root of this colorful, if not tacky phrase, is believed to have originated with an African witchdoctor in the service of the infamous Zulu king, Shaka Zulu, whose interpretation of Shaka's fecal deposits had repeatedly forewarned of impending doom for many of Shaka's enemies—indicated by his large, straight droppings.

While reading goat entrails is the more common method of divining the future among the Zulu people today, those who live by the old ways continue the "poop reading" tradition established by Shaka's auger.

Large, straight turds are generally viewed as good omens for an individual—indicating, at a minimum, no need to worry about constipation—which is always good news!

Brought to America by the British of South Africa, the expression has taken on a purely figurative meaning today—although there are rumors of a growing curiosity among fortunetellers as to its accuracy!

Sweep it under the rug:

Today a euphemism commonly meaning to pretend an incident never occurred, the habit of "sweeping under the rug" was actually a widespread practice in the United States and Europe until the invention of the floor sweeper in 1811.

As was the common method of floor sweeping, dirt was typically swept from the furthest points of the household toward the backdoor, and then swept outside. (The oldest remaining settlements in the United States attest to this fact by the large deposits of buttons, hair ornaments, pieces of broken glass and china, and other objects found in the dirt outside residential backdoors.)

In cold areas of the country, however, where snow fall was sometimes heavy and winters long lasting, it was often impractical and sometimes impossible to sweep out the back door, so piles of dirt and debris were simply swept under the rugs until spring thaw.

Many diaries of the Colonial period refer jokingly to the raised carpet bumps that crunched when walked over, stating, "I hope spring comes soon before I trip and fall and break my leg!"

Wise ass:

The number of "ass" expressions in American slang number in the hundreds. In fact, we have more references to ass (figurative and actual, anatomical and zoological) than any other single linguistic reference!

And while most don't seem to have any discernable origin, I was easily able to trace "wise ass" to 18th century Norfolk, Virginia, and the city's most famous (yet unknown) occupants, the Ass family: Wise and Tight Ass, their daughter Kiss (who went on to marry Jonathan Off), and their twin boys Lazy and Dumb.

THE BOOK OF ADAGES, APHORISMS, IDIOMS, AND COLORFUL EXPRESSIONS

Journal entries and newspaper clippings of the period show that while Wise was well-liked and respected in Norfolk society, Tight was generally considered a "pain," and never more than tolerated for Wise's sake.

Lazy and Dumb apparently quit school in the 4th grade and run off with a traveling side-show troupe. (Rumors say Dumb married 500 lb conjoined twins, while Lazy only lived up to his name, becoming known as the man with the world's longest toe nails!)

Daughter Kiss seems to have faired the best, having three brilliant though hard-hearted kids, Buzz, Fob, and Shove, all of whom went on to become successful attorneys, and then went into Washington politics!

You don't know shit from Shinola:

In most big cities of America during the early part of the 20th century, shoe-shine boys could be found on most every street corner.

All an enterprising young man had to have was an old rag—and not even a clean one—a horse brush, and an ample supply of saliva to start his own business. "Spit" shines went for $.05 cents.

But by the late 1920s, however, a number of commercially-made shoe waxes were being marketed, including *Shinola* brand show polish. So it wasn't long before the more discerning and better tipping customers insisting on a *Shinola* shine.

But even at $.25 a tin, using *Shinola* meant far less profit for the average shoeshine boy who may only get a handful of shines on a given day.

So, to combat the growing interest in commercial waxes, many boys started to improvise: *yes*, they resorted to using manure! They'd buy an old, used *Shinola* tin for $.02 from another, more fortunate kid, pack it full of horse or cow manure, and proceed to take care of their customers as usual—with few ever, apparently, catching on!

Thus, a common expression among shoeshine boys of the times was, "Ahhh! He didn't know *shit* from *Shinola!*"

Don't look a gift horse in the mouth

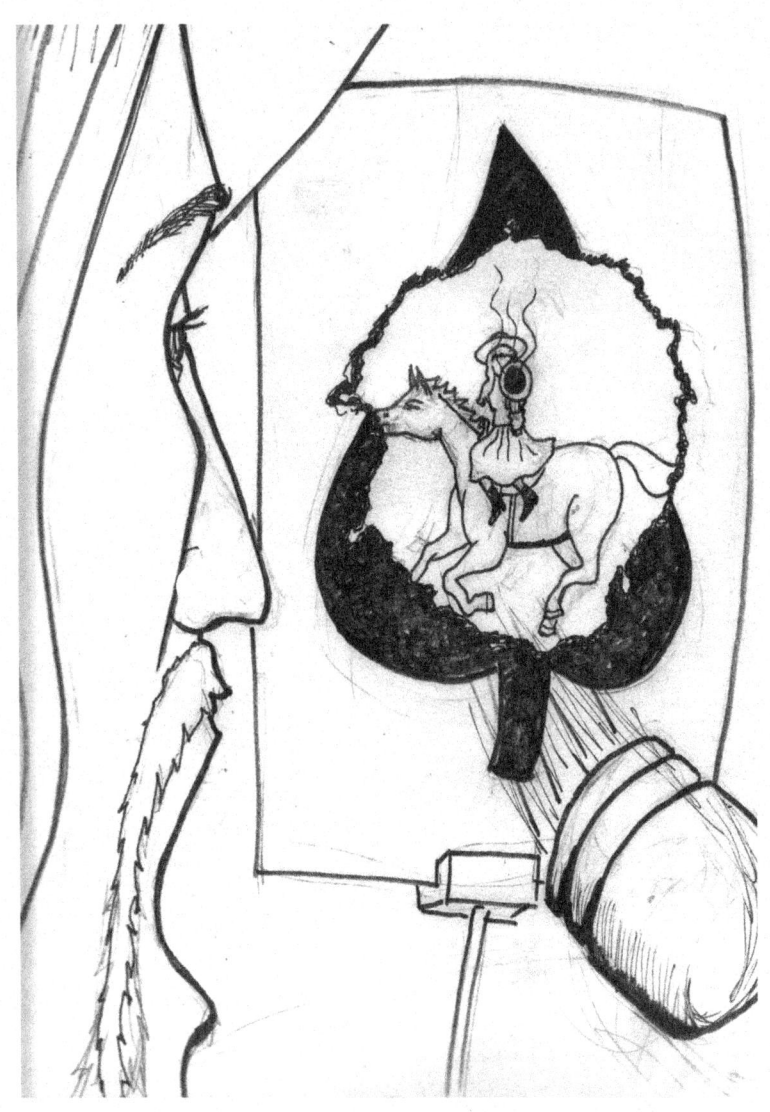

That hit the spot

Drunk as a skunk

Nose to the grindstone

Don't give me no lip

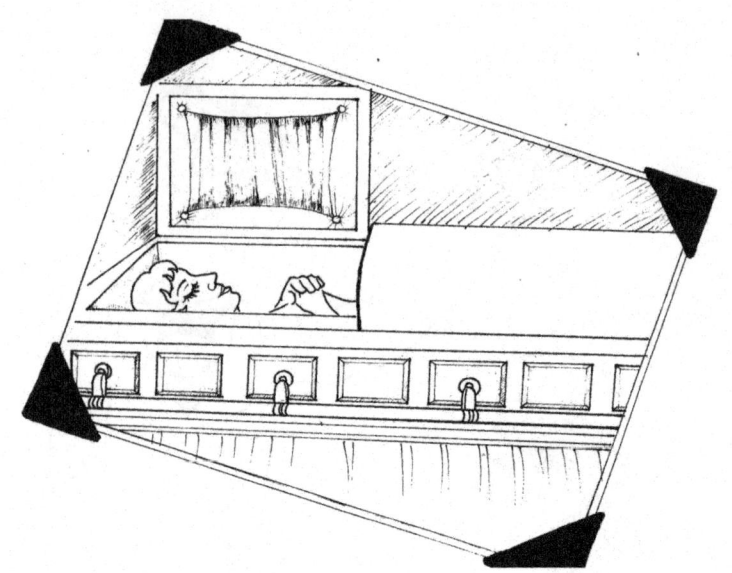

Pretty as a picture

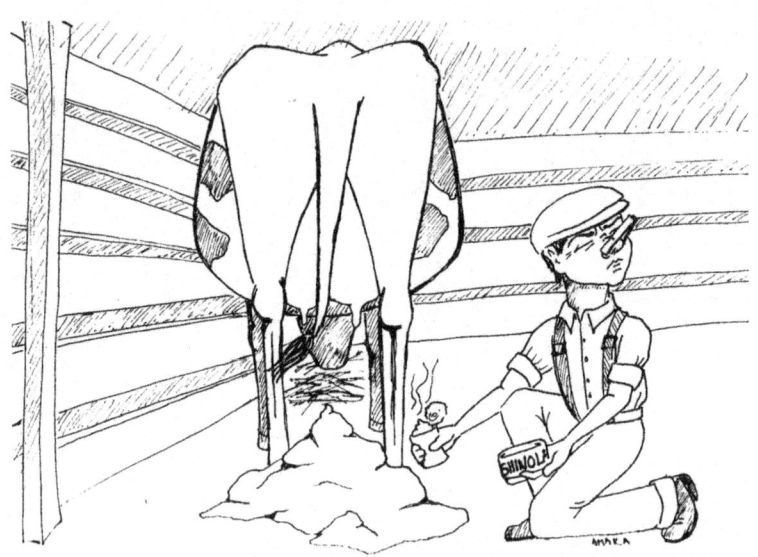

(You don't know) shit from Shinola

Between you and me and the fencepost

Knee-high to a grasshopper

Stink up a storm

Bone up

Don't get your tits tangled

(A) shit and two are eight and a fart is a fraction

CHAPTER FOUR:

"Fractured Fables"

In the telling and retelling of classic fables and faery tales, these traditional stories typically evolve over time, with many variations popping up culture to culture.

What may start out as a traditional folktale from Arabia, may resurface in France a century later, with each culture having added its unique cultural flavor.

And as history will attest, what may be fitting for one era and cultural setting may be quite inappropriate or even offensive during another—and sometimes, makes no sense at all without the cultural framework.

Through this process, a number of colorful phrases have become part of modern English vernacular, with few who use them actually knowing the cultural connection or literary source.

Between you and me and the fence post:

Before being adapted to the silver screen, L. Frank Baum's original fantastic tale, *The Wonderful Wizard of Oz,* was a much different tale than we've become accustomed to.

In the original version, for example, the Scarecrow, Tin Man, and Lion played much less significant roles. While each character added key components to Dorothy's extraordinary adventure, each ultimately had faults which prevented them from completing the journey to Oz with her.

The Tin Man, for instance, was so obsessed with chopping down trees that he kept side-tracking Dorothy from the yellow brick road—and finally had to be left behind (with Dorothy acknowledging that he would surely end up rusted in place again because of his arboreal obsession).

The Lion, too afraid to even leave the safety of the forest and accompany Dorothy to Oz, also had to be left behind, in the end, doomed to his own insecurities.

And as Dorothy quickly found out at the start of her journey, the Scarecrow was simply too neurotic to want along at all. Apparently having spent far too much time nailed up on that post in the cornfield, Scarecrow had come to believe that the corn, the fencepost, and even the straw in his head were alive—and he couldn't wait to escape them!

Though this plot development didn't survive the transformation to film, one of Scarecrow's biggest lines in the

THE BOOK OF ADAGES, APHORISMS, IDIOMS, AND COLORFUL EXPRESSIONS

book was, "Well, Dorothy, between you and me and the fence post, I think the corn and the crows are plotting against me!"

Realizing the Scarecrow had surely lost his mind, Dorothy ignored his request to help him down off the pole, and figured it was actually the safest place for him!

(You) bet your ass:

Though many accounts of this ancient tale exist throughout the world, the Sanskrit version attributed to 3rd century BCE India is said to be the oldest.

According to this parable, three brothers, Pingalaka, Sanjivaka, and Karataka, left their family home to seek their fortune to the north, beyond the great valley.

Taking just their clothes, tools which their father had given them, and sacks of food their mother had prepared for them, they loaded their donkeys and set off.

After only a few days' journey, they came upon a wondrous riverbed which, to their amazement, was covered with large nuggets of glistening silver. And when they looked up the mountainside, they saw a large silver vain so rich that it nearly blinded them in the sun. Rejoicing arm-in-arm, they happily hurried up the mountain to claim their prize.

Dumping out all the food their mother had prepared for them, the three used the tools their father had given them and hurriedly filled sacks. All that day and the next they loaded their bags, feeling quite pleased with themselves, giddy as they worked.

By the third day, however, when hunger and weakness began to overtake them, they started to regret having been so hasty with their mother's gift of food.

It was at this time that the youngest brother, Karataka, revealed that he hadn't thrown all of his food away. In fact, he'd kept one full sack which he'd tied high in the branches of a shady tree.

"Well, share it!" demanded Pingalaka, the eldest of the three.

Quickly considering his position, Karataka said, "Well, if you hadn't been so greedy for silver, you would have saved some food, too!"

"I demand that you share!" said Pingalaka.

"I will not!" said Karataka. "I have only enough to see me down the mountain and home again!"

Scheming with his older brother, Sanjivaka, the middle brother said, "How about we play a game of chance for your food? If you win, you keep your food and one sack of silver from each of us, which we will gladly carry back down the mountain for you. If you lose, you give us your food and we will owe you nothing."

Karataka thought for a moment and then conceded.

Playing a simple game requiring each player to choose which clinched hand a pebble is being held, the crafty older brothers

THE BOOK OF ADAGES, APHORISMS, IDIOMS, AND COLORFUL EXPRESSIONS

were able to not only trick Karataka out of his food, but quickly won much of his silver as well.

Finally figuring out how they were tricking him, Karataka said, "Shall we play more?"

Not believing their luck (or their little brother's stupidity), the older two said, "Sure! We'll give you the chance to win back your silver!"

To this Karataka said, "No, I do not wish to play for your silver, but will play for your asses."

In disbelief at their brother's foolhardiness, Sanjivaka said, "You would wager your silver against our flea-bitten asses?"

Karataka said, "Yes! You bet your asses!"

The three shook hands.

Now wise to their method of deception, Karataka quickly won both their asses. He now had half the silver he started with and all three asses.

"Foolish Karataka!" the elder brothers laughed. "You have lost half your silver and still you seem happy! We have taken your food and kept all our silver! You are truly foolish beyond all fools!"

To this Karataka replied, "Perhaps. But how will you now get your silver off the mountain?!"

(Wearing your) birthday suit:

In the commonly-known version of the famous Hans Christian Andersen tale, "The Emperor's New Clothes," two devious weavers promise to make the Emperor a new suit of very special clothes. Clothes, they say, that are only visible to those fit and competent for their social positions.

Believing the two crafty tailors, the slow-witted Emperor is seen a short time later proudly parading down the street before his loyal subjects in his new outfit, prompting a child in the crowd to cry out, "But he isn't wearing anything at all!"

But if we trace this story back a century to the Far East, we discover a somewhat different version of this cautionary tale.

In an older rendition originating in India, a Raja is seeking a new gown for his grand 80th birthday gala, to which everyone in the kingdom will be invited.

In this telling, with all his loyal subjects in attendance at the palace, as the Raja mingles with his people, shaking hands, the littlest subject yells out the more culturally relevant, "Gee, I didn't know you get white hair down there *too* when you get old!"

The idea of your birthday suit being the suit you were born with stems from this tale (as well as the phrase "Out of the mouths of babes")!

THE BOOK OF ADAGES, APHORISMS, IDIOMS, AND COLORFUL EXPRESSIONS

Bosoms 'til Tuesday:

In the original 17th century French version of the Disney classic, *Cinderella*, as Cinderella impatiently paces the floor waiting for her Prince Charming to arrive with glass slipper in hand, she begs her faery godmother to favor her with another tap of her magic wand—well, *two,* actually—just to help cinch the deal! (Seems man's obsession with the female bosom isn't such a new phenomenon!)

Unfortunately for both Cinderella and her Prince Charming, however, like the pumpkin carriage and footmen, all the faery godmother's spells had time limits! (This may also be the source of the term, "False advertising.")

While several early film versions of the *Cinderella* story included this sweet and charming scene, Walt Disney ultimately decided it was too risqué for young 20th century American audiences!

Bull feathers/horse feathers:

According to Classic Greek mythology, at the beginning of time when the gods first created the earth from Chaos, a number of animals initially shared the heavens with the first great birds. Horses (pegasi), unicorns, dragons, griffins, and of course, bulls—the most sacred animal of the ancient Greek gods—were frequently seen soaring high above.

But with so many great beasts cruising the skies, it was virtually impossible for earthlings to venture out into the open for fear of being bombarded with giant-sized animal droppings—which the gods in their irrepressible senses of humor, found hilarious! (Uranus and Gaia often wagered on which earthling would get splattered next!)

After repeatedly petitioning the gods to clip the wings of these giant scat-makers—which only send the gods into fits of uncontrollable laughter—the earthlings decided to take matters into their own hands by stealing handfuls of feathers from the beasts each time they descended to earth to feed. Eventually, featherless and unable to take flight, these creatures became earth-bound, where they remain to this day.

While few believe this ancient myth is in any way based in reality, it is said that the National Archaeological Museum in Athens has a secret collection of bull feathers stored in an airtight, hermetically sealed vault!

Caught red handed:

Perhaps no faery tale in history has undergone more transitions through the ages than *Little Red Riding Hood*.

With numerous storylines evolving, various versions have portrayed not only the Big Bad Wolf as the villain, but also Grandma, the Woodsman, and even Red herself.

In one of the more bizarre renditions, we find that Red is having an ongoing love affair with the suave and debonair Wolf, but then catches him in bed with Grandma when she pays an unannounced visit on the supposedly ailing old woman!

THE BOOK OF ADAGES, APHORISMS, IDIOMS, AND COLORFUL EXPRESSIONS

Upon discovering the two *in flagrante delicto* (Latin for *red-handed*), Red attacks the two with an axe in a fit of jealous rage, bludgeoning the Casanova Wolf before turning her weapon on Grandma! If not for the Woodsman who happens by and neatly chops off Red's head, she surely would have ended Grandma's life right then and there!

With the Big Bad Wolf and Red out of the picture, this version ends with Grandma and the Woodsmen shacked up in her secluded cottage, living happily ever after!

While this rendition was updated to serve modern sensibilities, the term "red handed" remains a favorite expression even today!

Chip off the old block:

One of the most beloved storybook tales of all time, the 1883 tale of *Pinocchio,* the boy created out of wood by the woodcarver Geppetto, has undergone many transformations since its conception.

In the original telling, *Pinocchio* was the bitter-sweet story of a boy carved from wood because a woodcarver and his wife had no children of their own and were growing lonely in their old age. A fateful day arrives, however, when Pinocchio realizes that he is only made of wood and that no one could ever really *love* him because he can't do what real boys can do. But, Geppetto and his wife convince Pinocchio that they love him just as much as if he were real, and just as much as if he was their own, because they had *chosen* him as their son. He was the creation of their dreams!

But then Pinocchio overhears his parents talking, admitting that he had actually been a "chip off an old block" of wood; a wood-working blunder that almost became firewood!

In one of the final, heart-wrenching scenes, Pinocchio exclaims, "So, I was just a mishap!? A fluke! You lied! You didn't really *want* me! You didn't really *choose* me! I was...I was...an *accident of birth*!"

Finding this ending poignant but ultimately too sad, later writers followed a different storyline, though the phrase "chip off the old block" managed to survive the ages all the same!

Even steven:

The long lost Hans Christian Anderson story of "Even Steven and Odd Todd" is thought by many literary historians to have been Anderson's finest and most ambitious work after "Thumbelina"—even though no remaining manuscript survives.

Written late in life, the tale centers around two highly competitive brothers, one of which believes it's far better to speak and do everything in even measure, while the other, believes it's best to favor odd!

Set in the Danish hamlet of Odense, Steven and Todd are weaver's apprentices to their father, the village tailor, an aging man whose eyesight has grown too poor to any longer thread the needle. As the only tailor for over one hundred miles, all the villagers are depending on Steven and Todd to master their father's sewing skill.

But with Steven only willing to speak, walk, eat, and perform his tailoring in even measure, and Todd only willing to perform in numbers odd, their father quickly realizes that if the two are to assume the family profession, they must work in tandem, each complementing the other.

But what their father doesn't know is that neither Steven nor Todd intends to concede control to the other brother—believing their rhythm superior to the other—each secretly planning to permanently eliminate his brother once they've mastered their father's art!

Although no one knows how this story ends or how Anderson resolved the opposing issue, the expression "even steven" survived the centuries and can be heard in countless settlings across the US on any given day!

Go suck a toad:

While most everyone knows the story of *The Frog Prince*, the Brothers Grimm literary classic of the prince who was turned into a frog by a wicked witch, then magically transformed back to a human by the kiss of a princess, most are unaware that in the original version, the plot followed a somewhat different zoological path.

As the story goes, while penning the original yarn, Wilhelm, the younger and more assertive Grimm brother (rumored to have been half insane), had insisted that the Princess be made to suck a toad.

Although Jacob, the older and more passive brother, found the idea revolting—and the title *The Toad Prince,* ridiculous—he ultimately acquiesced to his little brother's wishes to keep peace in the family.

But foolish he was not.

Shortly after Wilhelm passed away, Jacob quickly revised the story, trading the toad for the frog.

Most literary historians agree that Jacob no doubt did the wise thing, and even contributed to making the kissing of frogs fashionable—at least in faery tales!

Hog Heaven:

One of the more difficult expressions to track down, I finally discovered that the term "hog heaven" is actually a contemporary expression coined with the founding of the institution of the same name.

Established by well-intended *Filmways*/CBS TV executives in honor of legendary television star Arnold Ziffel of *Green Acres* fame, "Hog Heaven" was an attempt to erase the black mark incurred by the TV industry after the ill-fated "Sow's Ear" episode which ended the popular and long-running show—as well as the talented porker's life!

THE BOOK OF ADAGES, APHORISMS, IDIOMS, AND COLORFUL EXPRESSIONS

Now extended to the film industry as well, recent inductees into "Hog Heaven" include the Three Little Pigs, Porky Pig, Babe, and *Toy Story*'s Hamm (which got broken during the filming of the most recent *Toy Story* installment).

(Insiders say Miss Piggy of the *Muppet Show* is already a shoe-in for induction when she reaches her final storyboard, which considering her dietary habits, won't be long now!)

R.I.P. Sir Arnold Ziffel: 1955 to 1971.

Just because there's snow on the roof, doesn't mean there's no fire in the furnace:

There can be little doubt that it was none other than Jolly Old St. Nick himself who first pointed out this reality about himself—and of aging!

But what discerning minds still want to know is, since Mrs. Clause already knew of Santa's *randy* side, who was he trying to impress—or entice—with this seductive declaration?!

(Rumor has it that Santa's head elf, Dooley, has the inside scoop, but is prepared to take it to his grave!)

Knee-high to a grasshopper:

After tracing the classic *Tom Thumb* folktale back centuries to one of its earliest incarnations, we find a storyline in which Tom's father attempts to comfort the tiny Tom by telling him that he too was quite small as a boy—standing no taller than "knee-high to a grasshopper"—before *shooting up like a weed*!

Years later, however, after Tom had experienced a wild sex quadrangle with Princess Huncamunca, the giantess Glumdalca, and King Arthur's wife, Queen Dollalolla (all of whom were turned on by his diminutive *size*), after having had brief flings with both Thumbelina and Thumbling—and both at once!—Tom ultimately feels sorry for his old man who has had only one sex partner in his whole life because of his unfortunate size!

"If only you'd *stayed* knee-high to a grasshopper, Dad," Tom laments, "you could have had a life worth talking about!"

No shit, Sherlock:

As I stumbled upon while reading Arthur Conan Doyle's recently discovered collection of lost tales, this cutting phrase was actually the startling discovery made by Holmes' friend and closest confidant, *dear* Watson, during the attempted solving of the "Case of the Missing Cowpie," Sherlock Holmes' most baffling and anything but elementary case!

(He never forgave poor Dr. Watson for not finding one to step in!)

Without *shit* to connect the prime suspect to the crime, the case remained unsolved, thus ruining Holmes' perfect record and flawless reputation, and subsequently making him the laughing stock of Scotland Yard for the reminder of his drunken, drug-addled career!

THE BOOK OF ADAGES, APHORISMS, IDIOMS, AND COLORFUL EXPRESSIONS

Only a paper moon:

One of the most bitter-sweet tales of romance and tragedies ever known is the story of Carmelita and Carlos, two love-struck prisoners of war who meet while in prison in 1847 during the Mexican-American War.

Occupying adjoining cells for six months while awaiting sentencing, the gentle Carlos falls in love with the beautiful but delicate Carmelita, vowing to wait for her no matter how long it takes.

Carlos, who was imprisoned for not paying his taxes, is unaware that Carmelita was jailed for murdering a Colonel in the French army and is destined for the gallows—a fact she keeps secret.

Finally, the day arrives when Carlos is freed.

Determined to keep his promise to Carmelita, one starless night shortly after his release, Carlos sneaks onto the prison grounds hoping to see his beloved through her window. As he reaches a spot under her cell, he hears her sadly lamenting, "If only I could once again see the moon in all its splendor, I would be a happy women. This is all I ask, guardian angel, just to see the moon one more time!"

Realizing for the first time that Carmelita can only see the wall across the prison yard from her window, Carlos decides to make his sweetheart's dream come true.

Returning the next night at dusk with a paper moon painted silver attached to a long pole, Carlos raises the moon to the bars just as darkness falls. A moment later his heart begins to sing as he hears his beloved say, "Oh, guardian angel, you have heard my prayer! I see the moon that you have brought me! Now I am a happy woman!"

Thrilled that he has brought his sweetheart such joy, Carlos returns night after night, each time raising the paper moon just as darkness falls; each night rejoicing as she thanks her guardian angel.

But then one night upon arriving at the usual time, Carlos raises his paper moon but hears nothing. Holding it in place until he thinks his arms will surely break, he waits and waits, but hears nothing still.

Then suddenly a sound comes from behind him.

Turning around, Carlos sees Carmelita being led up the stairs to the gallows by four prison guards. Rushing to her, he calls out, "Carmelita! Here! The moon has risen for you! The moon has risen just for you!"

To this Carmelita replies, "Damn, you really are such a sap! Get a life, Carlos! Don't you think I know it's only a paper moon!" A moment later the trap opens beneath her and all Carlos' dreams are dashed to the ground!

(The) proof is in the pudding:

One of the more popular sayings of recent decades, this phrase was actually the utterance of the illustrious Chinese-

THE BOOK OF ADAGES, APHORISMS, IDIOMS, AND COLORFUL EXPRESSIONS

American detective, Charlie Chan, during the solving of one of his more baffling murder cases.

It seems that while paying a visit on Chan's #1 suspect, one Mr. D. B. White of London, Brussels, and Calcutta, his host served the famous criminologist bread pudding and English tea.

A moment later Chan whispered self-assuredly to his Number-One-Son, Lee Chan, "Look! Proof in pudding! Fat black worms in humble desert to poison honorable Chan! Must be murderer!"

(It's important to understand that at that time raisins were as yet unknown in Hong King and Chan had mistakenly thought he'd uncovered a clumsy attempt to eliminate him from the case!)

Still, it made for charming dialog!

Rip, roaring drunk:

What would you do if you awoke after having been asleep for twenty years? Well, if you're Rip van Winkle, you'd head directly to the local tavern for a drink—that's what you do!

When Washington Irving first penned his now classic short story of the lazy Dutchman *Rip van Winkle* back in 1819, his initial draft had the parched and disoriented Winkle heading straight to the local inn after awakening from his twenty-year drowse.

Rather than face his wife and admit that he'd fallen for Henry Hudson's trickery, Rip proceeds to tell his remarkable tale at the local tavern where he is joined by all the other men of the village who are also trying to avoid their wives.

Quickly becoming a legend and role model for the men of the Catskills, getting "Rip" roaring drunk became the definition of having fun and the formal declamation that a man is not "hen-pecked" by his wife!

When Irving's own wife learned of the story line, however, and realized it would promote drunkenness and idleness in men all around the world, she took a stand for wives everywhere and forced him to change the plot—or spend his remaining days sleeping under a shade tree in the woods!

Obviously, he gave in!

Shoot the moon:

One of the most enduring Native American tales of all time is the parable of Crazy Coyote and the Arrow from Heaven.

As the tale begins, Crazy Coyote, who until this time is called Wise Owl, is returning from a long day at the hunt when suddenly an arrow falls from the sky, landing at his feet. Looking up, Wise Owl sees nothing above but Mother Moon rising in all her radiant glory.

Believing the arrow belongs to his celestial mother—who may need it to defend the heavens—Wise Owl picks up the arrow and attempts to return it by shooting it at the moon. But time and time again, the arrow simply drops back to earth. Drawing his bow until all his strength is spent, he finally gives up in the morning when Mother Moon gives way to Father Sun.

Feeling it is his sacred duty to return the errant arrow, Wise Owl returns to the same spot the next night, and just as Mother Moon appears, he again attempts to return the arrow. But time and again—no matter how far back he draws his bow—it fails to reach its target and simply returns to earth.

For the next three nights, Wise Owl—who is now called Crazy Coyote by his people—returns to the same spot, determined to return the arrow, his disappointment growing greater and greater as his target grows ever smaller. Finally forced to give up when Mother Moon no longer rises into the heavens, Crazy Coyote decides to go in search of special wood with which to build a more powerful bow.

All day, everyday, for the next two weeks, he fashions bows, each more powerful than the one before. No longer does he perform his duties for his people. No longer does he care for his wife and children. No longer does he share in his people's sacred ceremonies. He can think of nothing but his quest to return the defiant arrow.

Now armed with a bow nearly as long as he is tall, made from five special woods, Crazy Coyote stood in his spot, waiting anxiously for Mother Moon to reappear, knowing it is her time.

Just then, a brave from a neighboring tribe happened by and sees Crazy Coyote standing with his bow and arrow poised. A broad smile comes to his face as he hurries up and says, "Ah, cool! You found my arrow! I've been looking all over for that!"

Living up to his new name, Crazy Coyote ran howling into the woods, never to be heard from again—except from afar!

Stink up a storm:

To get to the root of this unseemly expression, I turned to traditional Slavic folklore and the legend of Baba Yaga, the Russian hag said to fly through the air in a boiling caldron, live in a log cabin that moves around on chicken legs, and whose front door keyhole is a human mouth—complete with razor-sharp teeth!

While many literary historians compare Baba Yaga to other witches of popular lore because to her ability to affect the weather, there is actually one distinctive difference in her methodology; one that directly ties her to this colorful, if not distasteful, expression.

Unlike legendary witches of the West who conjure lightening and thunderbolts using spells and magic wands, Baba Yaga is said to cause tempests, hurricanes, and tornados merely by the powerful stench she expels! Often depicted with her rear-end extended, it is said that she can literally "stink up a storm"!

And according to some versions of this popular folktale, the sickening smell she gives off is due to her habit of dining on rotten children!

THE BOOK OF ADAGES, APHORISMS, IDIOMS, AND COLORFUL EXPRESSIONS

Talk is cheap:

Most everyone is familiar with the tale of *Arabian Nights*, the story of Scheherazade and the Persian Sultan Shihryar, in which night after night the new queen regales the king with exotic tales while he waits for her to finish so he can consummate their marriage and then put her to death like all the brides before her.

But in the original version, instead of sitting night after night hanging onto Scheherazade's every word—for 1,001 nights, in fact—after only the 3rd night, King Shahryar loses patience and abruptly interrupts Scheherazade in mid-story declaring, "Blah, blah, blah! Talk is cheap—I want some action!" At which point he has his way with her and then has her taken off to the swordsman for beheading!

Shortly after completing this rendition, however, the ancient storyteller apparently realized that no one would be captivated by a book called, *Three Nights*. Thus, 9998 more tales were added and a literary masterpiece was born!

Who let the cat out of the bag:

For many bookworms today, the name Mark Twain is most often associated with his series of books featuring the adventures of Tom Sawyer and Huckleberry Finn, which introduced such memorable characters as Becky Thatcher, Jim, Injun Joe, Aunt Polly, and Mary.

But what many readers are unaware of is that in his final days, Twain began work on at least two novels in which the character "Satan" was to be a pivotal player!

The Mysterious Stranger, as this final, unfinished novel was titled, was apparently worked on from 1890 until 1910, during which time Twain wrote multiple versions of the storyline. And it is in one such plot twist that the often repeated expression, "Who let the cat out of the bag" was first uttered.

As the story begins, we find Tom and Huck making their way through the swamps on their trusty raft, headed for the island where their old friend Jim the runaway slave has his secret shack. They've heard that Jim knows of a root potion that makes hair grow and both Tom and Huck feel it's time to grow a mustache!

When they reach the island, however, they find six squirming gunny sacks lying on the bank, which, of course, piques the two's natural curiosity. Upon opening the first bag, a large black cat suddenly leaps out—momentarily frightening the two boys speechless!

Suddenly, old Jim appears from the brush with a seventh squirming bag and upon realizing what Tom and Huck have done, cries, "No! Who let da cat out the bag?!"

Not understanding the consequence of their deed, Tom admits, "We let that dumb old pussy out! A right mean one, he was!"

THE BOOK OF ADAGES, APHORISMS, IDIOMS, AND COLORFUL EXPRESSIONS

Jim then explains that he had met up with "Satan" on the island, and to elude being caught, had turned himself into a cat! And since Jim didn't know which cat on the island was the right one—there were so many—he'd spent all night and day rounding up all the cats he could catch, intending to drown them in the bayou!

"You dast know what you boys done did!" Jim warns them. "You coulda freed da devil hisself!"

Although this novel is far less known than Twain's other fine works, the "cat out of the bag" expression seems to become only more popular with time.

CHAPTER FIVE:

"Naughty by Nature"

As with all languages of the world, the English language is filled with sexually-charges words and phrases; some quite crude and direct, others cute and just naughty by nature.

And one can't travel America or any other country around the world without encountering adages, euphemisms, and colorful expressions reflective of a culture's sexual attitudes and mores.

While some expressions lose their naughty nature over time and no longer reflect their risqué origins, others, no matter how many transitions they endure through the centuries, continue to remain naughty—almost as if by intent!

What would our language be without them!

THE BOOK OF ADAGES, APHORISMS, IDIOMS, AND COLORFUL EXPRESSIONS

Bend over backwards:

While the phrase "bend over backwards" has taken on a wholly figurative meaning in recent times, used to refer to an individual going above and beyond what would be considered sufficient, history shows that it's actually a reference to humankind's third culturally-recognized sexual position (after doggie and missionary), as depicted by African cave paintings dating back to 35,000 BCE

While early man undoubtedly tried every possible physical coupling to achieve coitus, as modern man can certainly attest, bending over backwards has both its obvious advantages as well as disadvantages—which is most likely why it didn't catch on and isn't commonly practiced in bedrooms (much) around the world today!

One additional historic note: As cave etchings seem to suggest, this position also appears to have made a female referred to as XOXO the world's first pin-up girl!

Black balled:

Although this sexual-sounding term has taken on an entirely non-sexual meaning in recent centuries, (that of being ousted from a group via the choosing of a black—vs. white—voting ball), in the brothels of ancient Babylon, it is said to have referred to a form of retribution used on men who were disrespectful to a harlot or refused to pay her.

As depicted on ancient cuneiform tablets, once such an ill-mannered client fell asleep (as men often do after sexual fulfillment), the woman would coat his testicles with indigo ink so as to mark him for other women, and perhaps, to announce his sexual activities to his wife or concubine.

Since indigo took several days to wear off, it became an inescapable social stigma for the man who attempted to procure sexual favors during his "black ball" period!

Once marked, many such men apparently chose to spend their black-balled time alone! (Seems there's some connection to the modern connotation after all!)

Bone up:

Among aficionados of the American Wild West, the legend of Red River Sarah is known far and wide.

Owner and operator of the first "gentlemen's club" in Miles City, Montana, Sarah was known as a woman who never said 'no,' and put more smiles on more men's faces than all the liquor, poker games, and dance hall girls in Montana combined.

Legend says her passions were insatiable, her sexual prowess, endless!

But that all came to a sudden end when the sultry Sarah met "Big" John Bighorn, chief of the local band of Lakota Sioux. Once the two met, Sarah was heard to utter a regretful 'no' for the very first time, and from that time on, send all her clients to Missy Julie, her younger cousin. And for the next forty years, Sarah gave all her insatiable desires to "Big" John and no one else.

THE BOOK OF ADAGES, APHORISMS, IDIOMS, AND COLORFUL EXPRESSIONS

But then one faithful day as John stepped out into the dusty street of Miles City, a most unfortunate event occurred; a runaway carriage driven by Miss June, the pastor's wife, hit and killed "Big" John dead where he stood. Sarah, of course, was devastated.

But even through her tears as the undertaker was measuring John for a pine box, the incomparable Sarah was heard to say, "Mr. Sullivan, do make sure you lay him in there *bone up*, now!" to which the undertaker is said to have given a quizzical look. "After all, by the time I meet my maker, I'm gonna be horny as a she-goat come springtime, and I don't wanna be wastin' no time havin' to roll him over!"

Cold as a witch's tit:

One of the more difficult *naughty by nature* expressions to track down, it seems this witty little saying actually belongs to none other than the famous conjurer extraordinaire, Merlin the Magician, and was apparently a simple attempt at colorful banter.

When asked by his host, King Arthur, how he liked his first summer spend in England, Merlin is said to have responded, "Cold as a witch's tit, Sire. Cold as a witch's tit!"

(I guess he would know!)

Cut to the chase:

While many believe this action-ready idiom originated in 20th century American filmmaking, suggesting jumping ahead to the scene where the inevitable *chase* occurs, I was able to find a much older historic—and naughty—reference for this expression.

As was customary among 10th century Norsemen, the courting process for a Viking involved several very public steps: First, a public declaration by the *hauld* (the hopeful groom), stating his desire to claim yon maiden as his own. Second, the subsequent public fight between the hauld and the ablest brother of the fair maiden in defense of her virtue. Third (if he survived), a public feast during which the hauld and his intended were honored at a betrothing feast during which massive amounts of food and grog were consumed. And finally, the very public traditional chasing of the maiden across the countryside, ending with the hauld permitted to tear off the maiden's *hangerock* and forcibly "take" his intended in traditional Viking fashion!

The problem was, relatively few actually survived the first three steps!

Thus, "cutting to the chase," was the wishful lament of the poor Viking who didn't fair well in his battle with the maiden's brother (losing an eye, arm, or perhaps worse), or passing out drunk before the chase could begin! Because in either case, he would be deemed unworthy to marry a Viking woman (other than, perhaps, an old, toothless hag), which would lessen his future chances of ever being accepted by a prospective father-in-law!

THE BOOK OF ADAGES, APHORISMS, IDIOMS, AND COLORFUL EXPRESSIONS

As was common Viking tradition, a man who couldn't fight, drink and eat to excess, and then ravage his woman, was considered no man at all!

Dick head:

The cultural custom of comparing an individual's head to the shape and/or appearance of other body parts, can be traced back centuries through the English language—and found in numerous other languages as well.

"Dick" head, "toe" head, "butt" head, and "skin" head are just a few such anatomical comparisons that have become popularized through the decades.

And although some cultures favor variations of the term *penis*, "dick" seems to have the most wide-spread appeal—perhaps because of the way it just seems to roll off the tongue so easily!

And as the old expression say, "If the shoe fits!"

Don't get your tits tangled:

According to Classic Roman mythology, these five well-chosen words of wisdom were the only advice Mars left with his twin sons Romulus and Remus as he deserted them on the banks of the Tiber River to be raised by a she-wolf.

(With Venus always on his mind, the hen-pecked Mars was apparently never really much of a father figure!)

Half past a monkey's ass and a quarter to his balls:

A quick review of the original Edgar Rice Burroughs novel, *Tarzan of the Apes,* published in 1914, shows us that this colorful phrase was simply "dinnertime" according to Tarzan and Jane's most reliable time piece, "Cheeta."

When the *Tarzan* epic made the jump to feature films, however, movie executives thought that while using a chimp (more specifically, his *anatomy*) to tell time was a rather quaint visual on the written page, the actual enactment would be just too bizarre—and perhaps, *frightening*—to see *larger-than-life* on the big screen!

This was unfortunate news, of course, for the first "Cheeta," a talented chimp named Bobo, who had already been trained to pose himself for "time-telling" every time the word *time* was mentioned—on or off the set! Invariably, it was a bad habit that wound up getting him replaced!

Bobo did, however make a fair living in later life, entertaining guests as *Cheeta* at countless Hollywood parties, willing to demonstrate his unique time-telling trick for a cheap cigar or girlie magazine!

Horny as hell:

Though commonly used today to describe a state of extreme sexual arousal, the underlying meaning of "horny as hell" to Appalachian men of 1800s Kentucky was an "unquenchable" sexual need, as one would surely suffer eternally in hell, where there is certainly no sex!

Since by their reckoning of the "good book" hell is a place where all the desires of man run rampant—lust among them—with no possible relief, everyone was "horny as hell" in hell, because sex didn't exist!

This belief is said to have provided many mountain men with the inner fortitude to resist temptation and remain on the straight and narrow—at least most of the time!

Just keep your pants on (You won't be here that long):

While I'm not making any personal confession here, I will say that if you're ever driving through Southern Nevada and pass by the infamous Chicken Ranch whorehouse, you can verify the origin of this expression for yourself!

Just inside the lobby is posted the list of house rules and regulations, of which this one is Number 3 and strictly enforced!

(Gotta wonder how it became such a commonly-used expression in the outside world, though, don't you?!)

(A) lick and a promise:

For the origin of this highly suggestive expression, we turn to the diary of the well-known womanizer Romeo, in which he describes his meeting with his hero and greatest inspiration, the infamous lothario, Casanova.

Upon meeting the notorious womanizer, Romeo asked what every other young man of the time was dying to know, "What is the secret of your sexual success?" To this the once common cunning linguist is said to have imparted knowingly: "A lick and a promise, lad. A lick and a promise!"

(You can draw your own conclusions!)

Lip lock:

As might be expected, official Church documents from Medieval Europe confirm that this highly intrusive and painful device is listed as the common companion piece for the popular sexual deterrent, the "chastity belt."

As historic documents show, when metal workers of the Middle Ages weren't hammering out armor for the kings' knights, many made substantial incomes devising evermore unbearable apparatus intended to preserve female virginity—which was, apparently, frequently in danger of being stolen, connived, or voluntarily surrendered.

These devices, which included breast cages, hand guards, and a thatched rear barrier, collectively constituted a veritable suit of impenetrable armor the weight of which most ladies were too fragile to even bear!

Thus, the lip and chaste devises were most often used when men had to leave their ladies unattended—spawning generations of master female lock pickers!

THE BOOK OF ADAGES, APHORISMS, IDIOMS, AND COLORFUL EXPRESSIONS

Pussy whipped:

Although "pussy whipped" is used today as a euphemism referring to a man who's *hen-pecked* or easily controlled by the allure of sexual reward, the term is actually a reference to the earliest known version of the cat o' nine tails, which did, in its original inception, actuality utilize the tails of nine cats!

Of course, with the term "pussy" used more often today to refer to female anatomy than the furry animal, and the cat o' nine tails becoming a regular fixture of a growing number of bedrooms, it's becoming harder and harder to be sure which type of "pussy whipping" is actually being referred to! Unless, of course, you're there!

(A) shit and 2 is 8 and a fart is a fraction:

This cheeky little expression is said to have been three-year-old mathematical genius Euclid's first mathematical calculation and matter-of-fact response to his long awaited first solo potty-chair achievement!

The famous Greek mathematician is said to have then gone on to calculate the arc, velocity, and trajectory of his pee stream!

(Every genius has to start somewhere!)

Shoot a beaver:

Perhaps no figure of the American frontier has garnered a greater legacy than Daniel Boone, and rightfully so.

Pioneer, folk hero, bare-knuckle brawler, member of the Virginia General Assembly—it seems only natural that such an iconic figure would have had not only his share of eager followers, but comely ladies as well!

Indeed, as documents of the period reflect, boys of the times wanted to be like him, and women wanted to be with him. He was the stuff of legends, epic poems, and folk songs!

But while Daniel Boone had apparently developed quite a reputation as a ladies' man back in mid 1700s Kentucky, it appears that much of that may have been purely a linguistic misunderstanding; a misunderstanding that evolved from the colloquialism, "shoot a beaver."

Seems it all began one spring afternoon when Daniel walked into town for a sack of coffee and a side of bacon, and stopped in at the local tavern for a mug of ale to wash down the trail. A group of boys had spied the coonskin cap-wearing Daniel enter and were anxious to hear about his latest exploits. Sneaking inside, they sidled up to Daniel at the bar.

When asked to share his recent adventures, Daniel mentioned to the eager boys that he'd shot and eaten a beaver the night before. Unaware that "shooting a beaver" was local slang for engaging in sex, the boys raced off to spread the word that Daniel had indeed bagged himself a woman the night before—which, of course, sent tongues to wagging as to which of the townswomen had given in to Daniel's manly charms!

From that time on, when Daniel would come into town, the boys would routinely run up and ask excitedly, "Shoot any beaver lately?" to which more times than not, Daniel would respond, "Sure did! Shot a bunch of 'em this week! And they was *goooood* eatin', too!" Which, of course, only added to his growing legend as a man who knew the ladies *well*!

Son of a bitch:

While in modern parlance this expression is meant as a demeaning insult implying that an individual's mother is as lowly as a dog, when used in its original form a millennium ago in Scandinavia, "Son of a She-Wolf" was an expression of utmost respect; the acknowledgement that an individual possessed the qualities of one of the most revered animals of the Germanic peoples.

Not only did the expression acknowledge that She-Wolf power and cunning coursed through your veins, but that your father had the physical strength and stamina to mate with one of the craftiest and fiercest beasts of all creation!

Even into the 18th century, being called a "son of a bitch" generally elicited the response, "Thank you, my friend! And I intend to take such a beast one day for myself!"

Stroke the mule:

A common colloquialism known to every boy over the age of ten in the US today, like *choke the chicken*, *spank the monkey*, and *charm the snake*, "stroke the mule" does, of course, refer to self-pleasuring. But unlike these other common animal references, "stroking the mule" has a somewhat different connotation and cultural reference.

Although mules are among the strongest beast of burden—and relied upon by American farmers for centuries—they are also infamous for their stubbornness. Once a mule sets its mind not to move forward, there is no known way to force them to. Well, *almost* no way.

As farmers of the mid-west discovered during pioneering times, male mules have one specific weakness: if you simply stroke his hindquarters, the animal will interpret it as a sexual advance, and once aroused will follow you pretty much anywhere you want to go!

Of course, having done so you're left with an *obviously* sexually-aroused 1000 pound beast of burden, but most farmers thought it a small price to pay to get their fields plowed!

Sympathy sex:

While not a common practice in the United States, in many other parts of the world, "sympathy sex" was and continues to be a cultural norm.

In many parts of the Eastern Europe, the Middle East, Asia, Southeast Asia, as well as among numerous tribes of South America, Africa, and islands off the coast of Australia, the loss of a wife is thought to be so devastating for a man to recover from that it has long been accepted behavior for single female members of the family to provide comfort by sleeping with him through a respectable period of grieving.

THE BOOK OF ADAGES, APHORISMS, IDIOMS, AND COLORFUL EXPRESSIONS

While it is common for sisters of deceased women to take on this role in many societies, other societies permit cousins and even village widows to assume this responsibility, and is considered a healthy way for a man to get over his loss and return the desire needed to seek a new mate.

In many languages, in fact, the terms "sympathy" and "consensual" derive from the same root word!

Tube steak:

Sausage, of course, has been a product of many European countries for centuries, invented and re-invented from culture to culture with each contributing its own unique selection of ingredients, processing, and serving tradition.

While German kielbasa and Scottish haggis vary greatly in content and cultural use, all in all, they're both *sausage*, and trying to expand on the general principle is no easy task.

But that doesn't mean there haven't been admirable and noteworthy attempts!

Wanting to create a variety of sausage that could be classified as strictly "American," colonial butcher George Alexander Jefferson decided to take the obvious physical similarities between the traditional sausage and that of male *genitalia*, and expand on the idea to create a commercial product.

Creating what he colloquially called a "tube steak," Jefferson came up with a phallus-shaped sausage stuffed with prime cured beef which was essentially the prototype for the American hot-dog.

The problem was, while all historical references to this culinary invention indicate that the tubular steak was actually quite tasty, men flat-out refused to be seen eating it, nor would they permit their wives to be seen purchasing them at Jefferson's butcher shop! (Of course, since the accompanying bun had yet to be invented, it probably was quite the comical if not shocking sight to see a consumer—man or woman—partaking of a penis-shaped sausage in a time when the mere sight of a man's bare chest sent women to their day bed with the vapors!)

In an effort to address the cultural sensibilities of the time, Jefferson apparently even offered door-to-door service to the hungry but squeamish, but his "plain brown wrapper" deliveries always caused a stir—even though back doors were usually utilized!

(Remember this the next time you see someone eating a hotdog!)

Wild hair up your ass:

While many contend that this is surely a literal reference to an often talked about incident involving a rather rambunctious rodent and a sleeping equine, I'm betting this phrase actually originated tens of thousands of years ago, as illustrated by a cave painting recently discovered in Kenya.

While it's impossible to be absolutely certain of what the ancient scene is depicting, it looks every bit as though a woman

THE BOOK OF ADAGES, APHORISMS, IDIOMS, AND COLORFUL EXPRESSIONS

is assisting a man in retrieving what appears to be an errant hair from the man's...*backside*! Presumably, a "wild" hair!

But, considering the body/hair ratio of our ancient brethren, I guess it should come as no real surprise that some hair would grow where we'd prefer they didn't!

Would you like to see your manuscript become a book?

If you are interested in becoming a PublishAmerica author, please submit your manuscript for possible publication to us at:

acquisitions@publishamerica.com

You may also mail in your manuscript to:

**PublishAmerica
PO Box 151
Frederick, MD 21705**

www.publishamerica.com

CPSIA information can be obtained
at www.ICGtesting.com
Printed in the USA
BVOW03s1204100817
491740BV00001B/12/P